THE MYSTERY OF
MRS BLENCARROW

Persephone Book N° 89
Published by Persephone Books Ltd 2010

The Mystery of Mrs Blencarrow was first published in 1890
and *Queen Eleanor and Fair Rosamond* in *Cornhill* magazine in
January and February 1886 and
in *The Widow's Tale* in 1898

Afterword © Merryn Williams 2010

Endpapers taken from a printed velveteen designed by
LF Day for Thomas Wardle & Co, sold by Liberty's in 1888
© Victoria and Albert Museum

Typeset in ITC Baskerville by
Keystroke, Tettenhall, Wolverhampton

Printed and bound in Germany by
GGP Media GmbH, Poessneck

9781903155790

Persephone Books Ltd
59 Lamb's Conduit Street
London WC1N 3NB
020 7242 9292

www.persephonebooks.co.uk

THE MYSTERY OF MRS BLENCARROW
and
QUEEN ELEANOR AND
FAIR ROSAMOND

by

MRS OLIPHANT

with a new afterword by

MERRYN WILLIAMS

PERSEPHONE BOOKS
LONDON

CONTENTS

THE MYSTERY OF
MRS BLENCARROW

CHAPTER ONE

THE BLENCARROW HOUSEHOLD

The house of Blencarrow, which, without being one of the great houses of the county, was as comfortable and handsome as a country gentleman not exactly of the highest importance could desire, stood in a pretty little park of its own, by the side of a bright little mountain river, either in Cumberland or Westmoreland or North Lancashire – for the boundaries of these counties are to me somewhat confused, and I cannot aver where one ends and another begins. It was built, as is not unusual in North-country houses, on the slope of a hill, so that the principal rooms, which were on a level with the great entrance, were on the other side elevated by at least one lofty storey from the flower-garden which surrounded the house. The windows of the drawing-room commanded thus a delightful view over a finely diversified country, ending in the far distance in a glimpse of water with a range of blue hills behind, which was one of the great lakes of that beautiful district. When sun or moon caught this distant lake, which it did periodically at certain times of the day and night, according to the season, it flashed suddenly into life, like one

1

of those new signals of science by which the sun himself is made to interpret between man and man. In the foreground the trees of the park clustered over the glimpses of the lively North-country river, which, sometimes shallow and showing all its pebbles, sometimes deepening into a pool, ran cheerfully by towards the lake. To the right, scarcely visible save when the trees were bare in winter, the red roofs of the little post-town, a mile and a half away, appeared in the distance with a pleasant sense of neighbourhood. But the scenery, after all, was not so interesting as the people inside.

They were, however, a very innocent, very simple, and unexciting group of country people. Mrs Blencarrow had been a widow for five or six years, having lived there for some dozen years before, the most beloved of wives. She was not a native of the district, but had come from the South, a beautiful girl, to whom her husband, who was a plain gentleman of simple character and manners, could never be sufficiently grateful for having married him. The ladies of the district thought this sentiment exaggerated, but everybody acknowledged that Mrs Blencarrow made him an excellent wife. When he died he had left everything in her hands – the entire guardianship of the children, untrammelled by any joint authority save that of her own brothers, whose names were put in the will as a matter of form, and without any idea that they would ever take upon them to interfere. There were five children, the eldest of whom was a slim girl of sixteen, very gentle and quiet, and not very strong; two boys of fourteen and twelve, at school; and two little ones, aged eight and nine respectively. They lived a very pleasant, well cared-for, happy life.

Mrs Blencarrow's means, if not very large, were comfortable enough. The house was handsomely *montée*, the children had everything they could desire; the gloom of her first widowhood had been over for some time, and she 'saw her friends' like any other lady in the county, giving very pleasant dinner-parties, and even dances when the boys were at home for their holidays – dances, perhaps, all the more gay and easy because the children had a large share in them, and a gentle licence prevailed – the freedom of innocence and extreme youth.

It is not to be supposed, when I say this, that anything which could in the remotest degree be called 'fast' was in these assemblies. Indeed, the very word had not been invented in those days, and Mrs Blencarrow was herself an impersonation of womanly dignity. The country people were even a little afraid of her, if truth must be told. Without being stiff or prudish, there was a little air she had, at the faintest shade of impropriety, which scared an offender more than denunciation. She had a determined objection to scandal, even to gossip, and looked coldly upon flirtation, which was not then a recognised pastime as it is now. Nothing ever filled the neighbours with greater consternation than when a passing visitor from London, seeing Mrs Blencarrow for the first time, declared that she was a woman who looked as if she had a history.

A history! When people say that, they do not mean anything noble or saintly; what it means is scandal, something that has been talked about. There was a general cry, which overwhelmed the unwary stranger. Mrs Blencarrow a history!

Yes, the very best history a woman can have – the record of a blameless life.

'Nevertheless,' said the unfortunate man, 'there is something in her eyes –'

'Oh yes, there is everything that is good in her eyes,' said Lady Tremayne, who was young and enthusiastic, a sentiment with which most of the others agreed. At a later period, however, Mrs Bircham, of The Leas, shook her head a little and said, 'Now that one thinks of it, there is something curious in Mrs Blencarrow's eyes.'

'They are very fine eyes, if that is what you mean.'

'No; that is not what I mean. She looks you too full in the face with them, as if she were defying you to find out anything wrong about her. Now, when there is nothing wrong to find out, a woman has no occasion to defy you.'

'It must be a strange kind of wrong that has not been found out in eighteen years.'

'Well, it might have happened before she was married – before she came here at all; and when you know that there is something, however long the time may be, you never can forget it, don't you know,' said Mrs Bircham, shaking her head.

'You seem to speak from experience, my dear,' said her husband.

'No; I don't speak from experience,' cried the lady, growing red; 'but I have seen a great many things in my time. I have seen so many fine reputations collapse, and so many people pulled down from their pedestals.'

'And helped to do it, perhaps,' said Lady Tremayne. But she made the observation in an aside, for no one liked to encounter Mrs Bircham's enmity and power of speech. She was one of those people who can develop a great matter from a small one, and smell out a piece of gossip at any distance; and a seed of this description sown in her mind never died. She was not, as it happened, particularly happy in her surroundings. Though she was irreproachable herself, there was no lack of histories in the Bircham family, and Kitty, her second daughter, was one of the little flirts of whose proceedings Mrs Blencarrow so much disapproved. Mrs Bircham was often herself very angry with Kitty, but by a common maternal instinct could not endure to hear from another any echo of the same reproof which she administered freely.

Mrs Blencarrow was, however, entirely unaware of this arrow shot into the air. She was still, though approaching forty, as handsome as at any period of her career, with all the additional charms of experience and understanding added to the still unbroken perfection of her features and figure. She was tall and pale, with large grey eyes, singularly clear and lustrous, which met every gaze with a full look, sometimes very imposing, and which always conveyed an impression of pride and reserve in the midst of their full and brave response to every questioning eye. Mrs Bircham, who was not without discrimination, had indeed made a very fair hit in her description of her neighbour's look. Sometimes those proud and steadfast eyes would be overbearing – haughty in their putting down of every impertinent glance. She had little colour habitually, but was subject to sudden flushes whenever her mind or feelings were affected, which wonderfully changed the character of her face, and came and went like the wind. She dressed always with a rich sobriety, in black or subdued colours – tones of violet and grey – never quite forgetting her widowhood, her friends thought, though always cheerful, as a woman with a family of children is bound for their sakes to be. She was an excellent woman of business, managing her estate with the aid of a sort of half-steward, half-agent, a young man brought up by her husband and specially commended to her by his dying lips. People said, when they discussed Mrs Blencarrow's affairs, as the affairs of women and widows are always discussed, that it would have been better for her to have had a more experienced and better instructed man as steward, who would have taken the work entirely off her hands – for young Brown was not at all a person of education; but her devotion to her husband's recommendation was such that she would hear of no change. And the young fellow on his side was so completely devoted to the family, so grateful for all that had been done for him, so absolutely trustworthy, that the wisest concluded on the whole that she was doing the best for her sons' interests in keeping Brown, who lived in the house, but in quite a humble way – one of the wisest points in Mrs Blencarrow's treatment of him being that she never attempted to bring him out of his own sphere.

Besides Brown, her household included a governess, Miss Trimmer, who bore most appropriately that old-fashioned educational name; and an old housekeeper, who had been there in the time of Mrs Blencarrow's mother-in-law, and who had seen her late master born – an old lady always in a brown silk dress, who conferred additional respectability on the household, and who was immensely considered and believed in. She came next to their mother in the affections of all the children. It was a very harmonious, well-ordered house, ringing with pleasant noise and nonsense when the boys came home, quiet at other times, though never quite without the happy sound of children, save when the two little ones, Minnie and Jimmy, were out of the way. As for Emmy, the eldest, she was so quiet that scarcely any sound of her ever came into the house.

Such was the house of Blencarrow on a certain Christmas when the boys had come home as usual for their holidays. They came back in the highest spirits, determined that this should be the jolliest Christmas that ever was. The word 'jolly', as applied to everything that is pleasant, had just come into use at school – I doubt even whether it had progressed into 'awfully jolly'. It sounded still very piquant in the ears of the youngsters, and still was reproved ('Don't be always using that dreadful word!') by mothers; the girls were still shy of using it at all. It was Reginald who declared it to be the jolliest Christmas that ever had been. The weather was mild and open, good for hunting, and the boys had some excellent runs; though all idea of frost and skating had to be given up. They were pleased with their own prowess and with everybody and everything round them, and prepared to act their part with grace and *bonhomie* – Reginald as master of the house, Bertie as his lieutenant and henchman – at the great ball which was to be given at Blencarrow on Christmas Eve.

The house was quite full for this great ceremonial. At Christmas the mixture of babes and grown-up young ladies and gentlemen is more easily made than at any other time of the year. The children mustered very strong. Those who were too far off to drive home that evening were with their parents staying at Blencarrow, and every available corner was filled. The house was illuminated all over; every passage and every sitting-room open to the bands of invaders – the little ones who played and the older ones who flirted – and the company was in the fullest tide of enjoyment, when the little incident occurred which I am about to record.

Mrs Blencarrow had never looked better in her life. She wore a new grey velvet dress, long and sweeping, without any of the furbelows of the time, which would not have suited the heavy material nor her own admirable figure. It was open a little at the throat, with beautiful lace surrounding the fine warm whiteness. Her hair was worn higher than was usual at the time, in a fashion of her own, and fastened with diamond stars. The children were very proud of their mother. She was like a lady out of a book, said Emmy, who was a romantic girl. Reginald felt himself more grand than words can say when he stood up beside her at the door to receive the guests. Her eyes were something like her diamonds – full of light; and she met every glance more proudly than ever, with that direct look which some people thought so candid and open, and Mrs Bircham believed to be a defiance to all the world to find out something that was not right. There was nothing, certainly, to find out in that open house, where every stranger might penetrate into every corner and welcome. Mrs Blencarrow was a little pale, but now and then her countenance would be covered by one of those sudden flushes of emotion which made her radiant. She put one hand on Reginald's shoulder with a proud gesture, as though he were supporting her as she stood at the door welcoming everybody; and the boy drew himself up to his fullest height, trying to look twenty. He shook hands with everyone in the most anxious, hospitable way. Never was the part of master of the house more thoroughly played; and thus, with every expectation of pleasure, the ball began.

CHAPTER TWO

'IS IT YOU?'

Kitty Bircham had been a flirt almost from the time she could speak; but even to a flirt fate sometimes comes in the midst of her frivolity, as well as to the simplest girl. She had played with so many hearts without being the worse for it, that it was the greatest surprise to herself, as well as to her mother and interested friends, to find that at last this little witch was herself caught. I need not say that the man was the last person whom, in her sober senses, Kitty would have chosen, or any of her family consented to. Man! He was not even a man, but a boy – only two or three years older than herself – a young fellow who had to go through one of those ordeals, quite new-fangled then – things which nobody understood – an examination for an appointment; and who had nothing in the world but the prospect of that, a prospect daily becoming less probable since he and she had fallen in love with each other. They were neither of them of that high strain which is stimulated by love. They had not force of mind to think that every day which was spent in love-making, quarrelling and folly made it less easy for Walter Lawrence to work the next, or to work at all; and that without work he was as little likely to pass his examination as to fly; and that if he did not pass that examination they could not marry.

Both of these young fools knew all this perfectly well, but the knowledge made no difference in their behaviour. When he was not running after her by his own impulse, which was generally the case, Kitty used all her wiles to draw him away from his books, sending him notes, making appointments, inventing ways and means of meeting. His mother made appeals to him with tears in her eyes, and almost cursed the girl who was making her boy lose all his chances; and *her* mother made Kitty's life a burden, asking her how she intended to live, and whether she meant to support her husband by her needlework (at which everybody knew she was so clever!), by taking in washing, or by what? – since he neither had a penny nor would ever be able to make one for himself. This discipline on both sides naturally threw these foolish young people more and more into each other's arms, and the domestic discomforts became so great that it at last became apparent to both that there was nothing for it but to run away.

'When we are married they will see that it is no use making a fuss,' Walter said to Kitty. 'They will acknowledge that once it is done it can't be undone.'

'And they *must* lay their heads together and get you a post, or give us something to live on,' said Kitty to Walter.

'They will never let us starve,' said he, 'after.'

'And they will never give us any peace,' said she, 'before.'

So that they were in perfect accord so far as the theory

went. But they hesitated to take that tremendous step; their minds were made up, and it was a delicious subject of conversation during the hours which they daily spent together; but neither of them as yet had quite screwed up courage to the sticking-point.

This was the state of affairs on the evening of the Blencarrow ball. It had happened to both to be unusually tried during that day. Kitty had been scolded by her mother till she did not know, as she said, 'whether she was standing on her head or her heels.' Her uncle, who had come from a distant part of the country for Christmas, had been invited to remonstrate with her on her folly. Papa had not said anything, but he had been so snappish that she had not known what to do to please him – papa, who usually stood by her under all circumstances. And Uncle John! Kitty felt that she could not bear such another day. Walter, on his side, had again had a scene with his mother, who had threatened to speak to her trustees, that they might speak to Walter to show him his duty, since he would not listen to her.

It was some time before this suffering pair could get within reach of each other to pour out their several plaints. Kitty had first to dance with half a dozen uninteresting people, and to be brought back demurely to Mrs Bircham's side at the end of every tedious dance; and Walter had to ask a corresponding number of young ladies before a happy chance brought them together out of sight of Mrs Bircham and Mrs Lawrence, who were both watching with the most anxious eyes. Kitty could not even lose time dancing when they had thus met.

'Oh, I have a dozen things to tell you!' she said; 'I must tell you, or I shall die.'

They went into the conservatory, but there were some people there, and into room after room, without finding a solitary corner. It was in the hall that the dance was going on. The servants were preparing the supper-table in the dining-room. The library was being used by the elder people (horrid elder people, always getting in one's way, who had no feeling at all!) for their horrid cards. The morning-room was given up to tea. People, i.e. other young pairs, were seated on the stairs and in every available corner.

'Oh, come down here; there is nobody here,' said Kitty, drawing her lover to the staircase at the end of a long passage which led down to the lower part of the house.

Both of them knew the house thoroughly, as country neighbours do. They had been all over it when they were children, and knew the way down into the flower-garden, and even the private door at the back, by which tenants and petitioners were admitted to Mrs Blencarrow's business-room. The lights were dim in these deserted regions; there was perfect silence and quiet – no other couples to push against, no spying servants nor reproachful seniors. The young pair hurried down the long stairs, feeling the cold of the empty passage grateful and pleasant.

'The old dining-room is the nicest place,' said Kitty, leading the way. This room was in the front of the house under the drawing-room, and looked out upon the lawn and flower-beds. It was part of the older house, which had served all the purposes of the Blencarrows in the days when people had not so many wants as now. There was no light in it except a faint glimmer from the fire. The shutters had not been closed, and the moon looked in through the branches of the leafless trees. The two lovers went in with a rush and sat down with quiet satisfaction upon a sofa just within the door.

'Nobody will disturb us here,' whispered Kitty with a sigh of satisfaction. 'We can stay as long as we like here.'

They were both out of breath from their rush; and to find themselves alone in the dark, and in a place where they had no right to be, was delightful. They sat quiet for a moment, leaning against each other recovering their breath, and then there happened something which, notwithstanding Kitty's intense preoccupation with her own affairs, gave her such a prick of still more vivid curiosity as roused every sense and faculty in her. She became all ear and all observation in a moment. There was a soft sound as of a door opening on the other side of the room – the side that was in the shade – and then after a moment a voice asked, 'Is it you?'

Walter (the idiot) suppressed with pain a giggle, and only suppressed it because Kitty flung herself upon him, putting one hand upon his mouth and clutching his coat with the other to keep him quiet. She held her breath and became noiseless as a mouse – as a kitten in the moment before a spring. The voice was a man's with something threatening in its tone.

'How long do you think this is going to last?' he said.

Oh, what a foolish thing a boy is! Walter shook with laughter, while she listened as if for life and death.

Then there was a pause. Again the voice asked anxiously, 'Is it you?' – another pause, and then the soft closing of the door more cautiously than it had been opened.

Walter rose up from the sofa as soon as the door was shut. 'I must get my laugh out,' he whispered, sweeping Kitty out into the passage. Oh, that foolish, foolish boy! As if it were a laughing matter! A man, a stranger, asking somebody how long 'this' was to last! How long what was to last? And who could he be?

'Oh, Wat, you might have stayed a moment!' Kitty said, exasperated; 'you might have kept quiet! Perhaps he would have said something more. Who could he be?'

'It is no business of ours,' said Walter; 'one of the servants, I suppose. Let's go upstairs again, Kitty. We have no business here.'

'Oh, don't be so silly,' cried Kitty; 'we must find a quiet place, for I've scores of things to tell you. There is a room at the other end with a light in it. Let us go there.'

Their footsteps sounded upon the stone passage, and Kitty's dress rustled – there could be no eavesdropping possible there. She went on a step in front of him and pushed open a door which was ajar; then Kitty gave a little shriek and fell back, but too late. Mrs Blencarrow, in all her splendour for the ball, was standing before the fire. It was a plainly-furnished room, with a large writing-table in it, and shelves containing account books and papers – the business-room, where nobody except the tenants and the work-people ever came in. To see her standing there, with all her diamonds flashing in the dimness, was the strangest sight.

'Who is there?' she cried, with an angry voice; then, 'Kitty! What are you doing here?'

'Oh, I beg your pardon, Mrs Blencarrow. We did not know what room it was: we couldn't find a cool place. Indeed,' said Kitty, recovering her courage, 'we couldn't find a place at all, there is such a crowd – and we thought the house was all open tonight, and that we might come downstairs.'

Mrs Blencarrow looked at them both with the fullest straight look of those eyes, whose candour was sometimes thought to mean defiance. 'I think,' she said, 'that though the house is all open tonight, Walter and you should not make yourselves remarkable by stealing away together. I ought, perhaps, to tell your mother.'

'Oh, don't, Mrs Blencarrow!'

'It is very foolish of you both.'

'It was my fault, Mrs Blencarrow. Don't let Kitty be blamed. I remembered the old way into the garden.'

'I hope you did not intend to go into the garden this cold night. Run upstairs at once, you foolish children!' She hesitated a moment, and then said, with one of her sudden blushes dyeing her countenance: 'I have got a bad headache; the music is a little too loud. I came down here for a moment's quiet, and to get some eau de Cologne.'

'Dear Mrs Blencarrow,' cried Kitty, too much unnerved for the moment to make any comments upon the lady's look or manner, 'don't please say anything to mamma.'

Mrs Blencarrow shook her head at them, looking from one to another, which meant gentle reproof of their foolishness, but then nodded an assent to Kitty's prayer. But she pointed to the door at the same time, rather impatiently, as if she wanted to be rid of them; and, glad to escape so easily, they hastened away. Kitty felt the relief of having escaped so strongly that she never even asked herself why Mrs Blencarrow should come down to the business-room in the middle of a ball, or if that was a likely place to find eau de Cologne. She thought of nothing (for the moment) but that she had got off rather well from what might have been an embarrassing situation.

'I don't think she'll tell on us,' Kitty said, with a long-drawn breath.

'I am sure she will not,' said Walter, as they ran up the long stone flight of stairs, and came back to the sound of music and dancing.

Mrs Bircham had just broken the monotony of a chaperon's vigil by taking a cup of tea. She was issuing forth from the door of the tea-room upon the arm of one of those portly old gentlemen who are there for the purpose, when Kitty, breathless with haste, pushing Walter along in front of her, suddenly came within her mother's view.

That mother's side Kitty did not again leave, save for the brief limits of a dance, all the evening. She read in the glance with which she was regarded from time to time the lecture that was in store for her. Indeed, she knew it all by heart; there was no novelty in it for Kitty. She gave Walter a despairing look as he passed her by, and they had time for a moment's whisper as to the spot where they must meet tomorrow; for all that she had intended to confide to him lay still in Kitty's heart unrevealed, and she began to feel that affairs had come to a crisis which demanded action at last.

CHAPTER THREE

AN ELOPEMENT

The ball was the most brilliant and the most successful that ever had been at Blencarrow, and nothing was wanting to make it intoxicating and delightful to the boys, whose every whim had been thought of and all their partialities taken into account. Mrs Blencarrow was perfect as a mother. She gave the young heir his place without showing any partiality, or making Bertie one whit less the beloved and favoured son of the house; and no one could say that she spoilt either of them, though she considered their every wish. They were as obedient and respectful as if they had been held within the severest discipline, and yet how they were indulged!

When everybody was preparing to go in to supper, Mrs Blencarrow called Reginald to her in sight of all the crowd. She said to him, 'I think you may go and fetch your friend Brown to supper, Rex. He will like to come to supper; but I am sure he will be too shy unless you go and fetch him.'

'Oh, may I, mamma?' said the boy.

He was enchanted with the commission. Brown was the young steward – Mrs Blencarrow's chief assistant in the management of the estate – the young fellow whom her husband recommended to her on his death-bed. The group which gathered round Mrs Blencarrow, ready for the procession in to supper, thought this was the most charming way of acknowledging the claims of Brown. To have brought him to the dance would have been out of place; he would have felt himself out of it. He could not have ventured to ask anybody to dance, and to look on while you are young is dull work. But to ask him to supper was just the right compromise. The old gentlemen promised to themselves that they would notice Brown; they would ask him to drink a glass of wine (which was the custom then); they would show him that they approved of a young man who did such excellent work and knew his place so well.

It must be allowed that when he came triumphantly led by Reginald, with Bertie dancing in front of him ('Oh, come along, Brown; mamma says you're to come to supper. Come along, Brown; here is a place for you'), his looks did not conciliate these country gentlemen. He was a handsome young man in a rather rough way, with that look of watchful suspicion so often to be seen on the face of a man who is afraid of being condescended to by his superiors. He was in a sort of evening dress, as if he had been prepared for the invitation, with a doubtful coat of which it was difficult to say whether it was a morning coat of peculiar cut, or an old-fashioned one for evening use. He yielded unwillingly, it seemed, to the encouragements of the boys, and he was placed far down at the other end of the table, among the children and the youngest of the grown-up party, where he was totally out of place. Had he been near the other end, where the honest country gentlemen were, quite prepared to notice and take wine with him, Brown would have been more at his ease. He cast one glance at his mistress as he passed, a look which was gloomy, reproachful, almost defiant. Scotch peasant faces get that look sometimes without any bad meaning, and Cumberland faces are very like the Scotch. He was no doubt upbraiding her for having forced him to appear at all.

At last it was all over, the last carriage rolling away, the last sleepy group of visitors sent to bed. Mrs Blencarrow stood on her own hearth, leaning her head on the marble mantelpiece, looking down into the fire. She had been very gay to the last, smiling upon her guests; but her face when in perfect repose, and in the ease of solitude, no one near to spy upon it, was very different. Anxiety and trouble came into every line of her fine pale features. She changed her attitude after a while, and looked straight into the darkness of the great mirror, behind the clock and the candelabra which stood in front of it. She looked into her own face with a determined, steady look, her eyes opened widely. She seemed to ask herself what she should do, but shook her head afterwards with a vague, sad smile. The mirror repeated all these changes of countenance, but gave no counsel. Someone came into the room at this moment, which made her start. It was one of the ladies staying in the house, who had forgotten something, and come back to fetch it.

'Not gone to bed yet?' she said.

'No,' said Mrs Blencarrow; 'after a business of this kind, however tired I may be, I don't sleep.'

'I know what you are doing,' said her friend. 'You are asking yourself, now that it's all over, "What's the good?"'

'No; I don't think so,' she said quickly; then changed her look and said, 'Perhaps I was.'

'Oh, I am sure you were! and it is no good except for such pleasure as you get out of it.'

'Pleasure!' said Mrs Blencarrow. 'But the boys liked it,' she said.

'Oh, the boys! They were more happy than words could say. I think you measure everything by the boys.'

'Not everything,' she said with a sigh; and, taking up her candle, she followed her friend upstairs.

The house had fallen into perfect quiet. There was not a sound in all the upper part; a drowsy stillness was in the broad staircase, still dimly lighted, and the corridor above; only a distant echo from below, from the regions which were half underground – a muffled sound of laughter and voices – showed that the servants were still carrying on the festivity. Mrs Blencarrow said good night at the door of her friend's room, and went on to her own, which was at the further end of the long gallery. She left her candle upon a small table outside, where it burned on, a strange, lonely little twinkle of light in the darkness, for half the wintry night.

Neither Kitty nor Walter could rest next day until they had eluded the vigilance of their several guardians and escaped to their usual meeting-place, where they poured into each other's ears the dire experiences of the previous night. Kitty had been badly scolded before, but it had been as nothing in comparison with what she had suffered on the way home and after her return. Mamma had been terrible; she had outdone herself; there had been nothing too dreadful for her to say. And papa had not stood by Kitty – the best that could be said for him was that he had taken no active part in the demolition of all her hopes.

'For I am to be sent away tomorrow to my aunt's in Gloucestershire – fancy in Gloucestershire!' as if there was something specially diabolical in that county.

'You shall not be sent away; the time has come for us to take it into our own hands,' said Walter soberly, with a strain of resolution.

He had to tell her of not unsimilar barbarities on his side. His mother had written to her trustees. She expected Mr Wadsett from Edinburgh, who was also her man of business (for her property was in Scotland), next day.

'Tomorrow is the crisis for both of us; we must simply take it into our own hands and forestall them,' said Walter. 'I knew that one day it would come to this. If they force it on us it is their own doing,' he said, with a look of determination enough to make any trustee tremble.

'Oh, Walter!' cried Kitty, rubbing her head against his shoulder like the kitten she was.

His resolute air gave her a thrill of frightened delight. Usually she was the first person in all their conjoint movements; to be carried along now, and feel it was not her doing, but his, was a new, ecstatic, alarming sensation, which words could not express.

They then began to consider without more ado (both feeling themselves elevated by the greatness of the crisis) what was to be done. Kitty had fondly hoped for a postchaise, which was the recognised way of romance; but Walter pointed out that on the railway – still a new thing in that district – there was an early train going to Edinburgh, which they could enter far more easily and with less fear of being arrested than a postchaise, and which would waft them to Gretna Green in less time than it would take to go ten miles in a carriage. Gretna Green was still the right place to which lovers flew; it was one of the nearest points in Scotland, where marriage was so easy, where the two parties to the union were the only ones concerned.

Kitty was slow to give up the postchaise, but she yielded to Walter's argument. The train passed very early, so that it would be necessary for her to start out of the house in the middle of the night, as it were, to join her lover, who would be waiting for her; and then a walk of a mile or two would bring them to the station – and then! Their foolish hearts beat high while they made all the arrangements. Kitty shivered at the idea of the long walk in the chill dark morning. She would have so much preferred the sweep of the postchaise, the probable rush in pursuit, the second postchaise rattling after them, probably only gaining the goal ten minutes too late. She had imagined that rush many a time, and how she might see her father or brother's head looking out from the window, hurrying on the postilion, but just too late to stop the hasty ceremony. The railway would change it all, and would be much less triumphant and satisfactory; but still, if Walter said so, it must be done, and her practical imagination saw the conveniences as well as the drawbacks.

Walter walked back with Kitty as near as he dared to The Leas, and then Kitty walked back again with him. They thus made a long afternoon's occupation of it, during which everything was discussed and over again discussed, and in which all the responsibility was laid on the proper shoulders, i.e. on those of the parents who had driven them to this only alternative. Neither of them had any doubt as to the certainty of this, and they had at the same time fair hopes of being received back again when it was all over, and nothing could be done to mend it. After this, their people must acknowledge that it was no manner of use struggling, and that it behoved them to think of making some provision for the young pair, who after all were their own flesh and blood.

Kitty did not undress at all, considering the unearthly hour at which she was to set out. She flung off her evening dress into a corner, reflecting that though it must be prepared after, instead of before, her marriage, she must have a trousseau all the same, and that no bride puts on again her old things after that event. Kitty put on her new winter dress, which was very becoming, and had a pretty hat to match it, and lay down to snatch an hour or two's rest before the hour of starting. She woke reluctantly to the sound of a handful of pebbles thrown against her window, and then, though still exceedingly sleepy and greatly tempted to pay no attention to the summons, managed at last to rouse herself, and sprang up with a thump of her heart when she recollected what it was – her wedding morning! She lighted a candle and put on her hat, studying the effect in the glass, though she knew that Walter was blowing his fingers with cold below; and then, with a fur cloak over her arm, she stole downstairs. How dark it was, and how cold! The country black with night, nothing visible but the waving, close to the house, of some spectral trees. But Walter pulled her hand through his arm the moment she slipped out, and her spirits rose. Two can face the darkness where one would shrink before it. They had the strangest, merriest walk – stumbling in the maddest way, jolting over stiles, going astray into ploughed fields, rousing all the dogs in all the farms and cottages for miles round – but at last found their way, worn out with stumbling and laughing, to the station, where the train had not yet arrived. And then came the rush and sweep through the night, the arrival in the grey morning at the station, the rousing up of the grim priest known as 'the blacksmith' – though I am not sure that this was his trade. Kitty found time to smarten herself up a little, to straighten the brim of her hat and put it on as if she had taken it fresh out of its bandbox, and to put on her white gloves – the only things truly bride-like, which she had put in her pocket before she left home – and then the ceremony, whatever it was, was performed, and the boy and girl were made man and wife.

After it was all over, Kitty and Walter looked at each other in the grey morning light with a pale and frightened look. When the thing was done the excitement suddenly failed, and for a moment everything was black. Kitty cried a little, and Walter, if it had not been for his pride of manhood, was very near following her example. What awful thing was it they had done? Kitty was the first to recover her courage.

'I am dreadfully hungry,' she said, 'and so tired. Walter, do go and see if we can have some breakfast anywhere. I must have some breakfast, or I shall die.' Kitty was very fond of this alternative, but had shown no intention of adopting it as yet.

'I'll go on to that public-house over there; but won't you come too, Kitty?'

'No; go and order breakfast, and then come and fetch me. I'll look over the books and see who have gone before us,' said Kitty.

He left her seated, half leaning over the table, studying the records which she had spread out before her. At that moment Kitty had a great sympathy for everybody who had been married, and a wondering desire to know what they had felt.

CHAPTER FOUR

A DISCOVERY

When Walter came back, having ordered a meal such as was most easily procurable in those regions, that is to say, tea and stale bread and fresh oatcakes and a dish of ham and eggs, he found Kitty waiting for him in a fever of impatience. She had one of the blacksmith's big register-books opened out upon the table, and her eyes were dancing with excitement. She rushed to meet him and caught him by the arm.

'Wat!' she said, 'oh, how soon can we get back?'

'Get back!' he cried; 'but we are not going back.'

'Oh yes, but we are, as quick as we can fly. Go and order the horses this minute – oh, I forgot, it's a train! Can't we have a train directly? When is there a train?'

'For goodness' sake, Kitty, what do you mean? But we are married! You can't be going to turn your back upon me.'

'Oh, fiddlesticks!' said Kitty, in her excitement; 'who talks of turning their back? I've found out something that will make mamma jump; it makes me jump to begin with!' exclaimed the girl, performing a dance on the floor. 'They'll never say a word to us. They'll be struck dumb with this. Look! look!'

27

Walter looked with great surprise, without the slightest conception of what it could be to which his attention was called. His eyes wandered along the page, seeing nothing. A long array of names: what could there be in these to call for all this commotion? Kitty pushed him aside in her excitement. She laid her finger upon one short signature written very small. He read it, and turned and looked at her aghast.

'Kitty! what do you mean? Who is it? It can't – it can't be –'

'Well!' cried Kitty, 'and who could it be? "Joan Blencarrow" – there's only one person of that name in all the world.'

'Good heavens!' Walter cried. He had more feeling than she had, for he stood aghast. Mrs Blencarrow! He seemed to see her suddenly in all her dignity and splendour, as he had seen her standing receiving her guests. Kitty jumped with excitement, but Walter was appalled.

'Mrs Blencarrow! I can't believe it! I don't believe it!' he said.

'What does it matter whether you believe it or not, for there it is?' said Kitty, triumphant. 'Oh, what a state mamma will be in! She will never say a word to us. She will pay no attention, any more than if we had been out for a walk. Oh, how she will like to pull down Mrs Blencarrow! – she that was always so grand, and people thinking there was nobody like her. And all this time – three years –'

Kitty's eyes danced with delight. To think that she should be the one to find out such a wonderful secret intoxicated her with satisfaction and pleasure.

'Kitty,' said Walter, with hesitation, 'we have found it out by accident.'

'Oh, don't say *we! I've* found it out. It would never have come into your head to look at the books.'

'Well, *you* then. You have found it out by accident, and when we're happy ourselves, why should we try to make other people miserable? Kitty!' He put his arm round her, and pleaded with his lips close to her ear.

'Oh, nonsense!' she said; 'all men are taken in like that; but I can't let her off; I won't let her off. Why, it wouldn't be right!'

'There are some people who would think what we are doing wasn't right,' said Walter.

'Oh, you coward,' cried Kitty, 'to turn round on me when we haven't been married an hour! As if it was my doing, when you know that but for you –'

'I am not turning round on you. I never said it was your doing. Kitty, darling, don't let us quarrel. You know I never meant –'

'I shall quarrel, if I like,' cried Kitty, bursting into tears; and they had it out, as they had already done a hundred times, and would a hundred more, enjoying it thoroughly. It suddenly occurred to Walter, however, as the little episode drew near a close, that the ham and eggs must be ready, and he threw in an intimation to this effect with very telling results. Kitty jumped up, dried her eyes, straightened her hat, and declared that she was dying of hunger.

'But whatever happens, and however serious things may be, you always will go on,' she said.

He was magnanimous, being very hungry too, and restrained the retort that was trembling on his tongue, that it was she who would go on; and they flew across to the little alehouse, arm in arm, and enjoyed their ham and eggs even more than they had enjoyed their quarrel.

They found out that the next train 'up' was not till eleven o'clock, which set their minds at rest, for they had meant to go to London before Kitty's mind had been all unsettled by that discovery. Walter had begun to hope she had forgotten all about it, when she suddenly jumped up from the table – not, however, before she had made a very satisfactory meal.

'Oh, what a fool I am!' cried Kitty. 'I never paid any attention to the man!'

'What man?'

'Why, the man she was married to, you goose! A woman can't be married all by herself. It was a long name – Everard something. I didn't know it, or I should have paid more attention. Haven't you finished yet? – for I must run this instant –'

'Where, Kitty?'

'Why, to look up the book again!' she cried.

'I wish you'd give this up,' said Walter. 'Do, to please me. We've got all we wish ourselves, and why should we worry other people, Kitty?'

'If you have got all you wish, I have not. I want to please them – to make them do something for us; and when a thing like this turns up – the very thing! – why, mamma will hug us both – she will forgive us on the spot. She'll be so pleased she'll do anything for us. I don't know about Mrs Lawrence –'

'It won't do us any good with my mother,' said Walter, with

a thrill of dread coming over him, for he did not like to think of his mother and that terrible trustee.

'By the way,' cried Kitty, with a pirouette of delight, 'it's I that am Mrs Lawrence now, and she's only the Dowager. Fancy turning a person who has always made you shake in your shoes into the Dowager! It's too delightful – it's worth all the rest.'

Walter did not like this to be said about his mother. He had deceived and disappointed her, but he was not without a feeling for her.

'That is all nonsense,' he said. 'It is not as if I had come into the property and my mother had to turn out; for everything is hers. I hope you don't mind being Mrs Walter, Kitty, for my sake.'

Kitty considered a moment whether she should be angry, but concluded that it was too soon after the last quarrel, and would be monotonous and a bore, so she caught up his hat instead and thrust it into his hand.

'Come along,' she said; 'come along. We have sat a long time over breakfast, and there is no time to lose; I must make out the other name in that book.'

But here the young lady met with an unexpected check, for the blacksmith stopped them as they entered his house, striding towards them from the kitchen, where he, too, had finished a very satisfactory meal.

'What will ye be wanting?' he said. 'Ye will maybe think I can unmarry ye again? but it's not possible to do that.'

'We don't want to be unmarried,' said Kitty; 'we want just to look at the book again, to see a name.'

'What book?'

'The register-book that is in that room,' said Walter; 'my wife,' and he gave Kitty's arm a squeeze, 'saw a name –'

'My book!' The blacksmith stood in the doorway like a mountain, not to be passed by or pushed aside. 'I'll have no one spying into the names in my book.'

'I don't want to spy,' said Kitty; 'it's somebody I know.'

But the big man would hear no reason; he looked at the little couple before him, so young and so silly, as if he had been a bishop at least.

'I couldn't refuse to marry ye,' he said; 'I hadn't the right. But if I had followed my own lights, I would just have sent ye home to your parents to be put back in the nursery; and ye shall see no books of mine, nor tell tales upon other folk.'

And nothing could move him from this resolution. Kitty nearly cried with vexation when they got into the train again; her own escapade dwindled into something quite secondary.

'It was so silly of me not to make sure of the name. I am sure the first name was Everard, or something like that. And what a brute that man is, Walter! If you had really loved me as you say, you would have pushed him away or knocked him down.'

'Why, he was six times as big as me, Kitty!'

'What does that matter,' she said, 'when it's for the sake of someone you love?'

But perhaps this is rather a feminine view.

There had been, as may be supposed, a great commotion in The Leas when it was found that Kitty's room was vacant in the morning. A girl's absence is more easily discovered than a boy's. Mrs Lawrence thought that Walter had gone off for the day to see some of his friends, and would come back to dinner, as he had done many times before; and though she was angry with him for leaving his work, she was not anxious. But a young lady does not make escapades of this sort; and when it was discovered that Kitty's best things had disappeared, and her favourite locket, and that she had evidently never gone to bed in a proper and legitimate way, the house and the neighbourhood was roused. Mrs Bircham sent off messengers far and near; and Mr Bircham himself, though an easy-minded man, went out on the same errand, visiting, among other places, Blencarrow, where all the gaiety of a Christmas party was still going on, and the boys were trying with delight the first faint film of ice upon the pond to see when it would be likely to bear. Then, after a hasty but late luncheon, he had gone to see whether Mrs Lawrence knew anything about the fugitive; and Mrs Bircham, at her wits' end, and not knowing what to do, was alone in the drawing-room at The Leas, pondering everything, wishing she had Kitty there to shake her, longing to pour forth floods of wrath; but at the same time chilled by that dread of something having happened which will come in even when a mother is most enraged. She was saying to herself that nothing could have happened – that it must be that young Lawrence – that the girl was an idiot – that she washed her hands of her – that she would have nothing to do with them – that, oh, if she had only thought to lock her up in her bedroom and stop it all!

'Oh, Kitty, Kitty! where are you, child?' she cried nervously at the conclusion of all.

There was a rustle and a little rush, and Kitty ran in, flinging herself upon her knees upon the hearthrug, and replied:

'Here I am – here I am, mamma!'

Mrs Bircham uttered a shriek. She saw Walter behind, and the situation in a moment became clear to her.

'You young fools!' she said; 'you disobedient, ungrateful children – you –'

'Oh, mamma, one moment. We have been to Gretna Green – Walter and me!'

'How dared you, sir!' said Mrs Bircham, turning upon the hapless lover – 'how dared you steal my innocent child away? And then you come here to triumph over us. Begone, sir – begone, sir, out of my house; begone out of my house!'

Kitty jumped up off her knees and caught Walter by the arm.

'He does not go a step without me,' she cried. 'But, mamma, if you would have a moment's patience, you would not think any more about it. We were going to London; but I came back, though I knew you would scold, to tell you. Listen to me one moment,' cried Kitty, running all the words into one; 'it's something about Mrs Blencarrow.'

Mrs Bircham had her hands raised, presumably to draw down the curse of heaven upon the pair, but at this name she paused; her countenance changed.

'Mrs Blencarrow?' she gasped, and could say no more.

'You never heard such a thing in your life!' cried Kitty. She dropped Walter's arm, and came forward in front of him. 'Mamma, I saw her name in the register; there it is – anyone can see it: Joan Blencarrow – there couldn't be another person with such a name.'

'In the register? What – what do you mean?'

'Mamma, I mean that Mrs Blencarrow is married – to somebody else. She's been married these three years. I read her name this very day. It's in the register at Gretna Green.'

Mrs Bircham staggered back a few steps and dropped into a chair.

'Married!' she cried. 'Mrs Blencarrow married!'

'Three years ago,' cried Kitty glibly. 'Fifth January – I saw the date – three years ago!'

Mrs Bircham sat with her hands clasped and her eyes glaring, 'as if,' Kitty said afterwards, 'they would come out of her head.' She uttered a succession of cries, from little shrieks to breathless exclamations. 'Married! – Mrs Blencarrow! Oh, oh, Kitty! Oh, good heavens! – Mrs Blencarrow! Three years ago – the time she went off to Scotland to see her sister. Oh, oh, Kitty! In the register! Get me a glass of water, or I think I shall die.'

Walter disappeared for the water, thinking that after all his mother-in-law was a good-hearted woman, and didn't feel as Kitty said she would; but when he returned, his admiration of Mrs Bircham turned into admiration for his wife, for Kitty and her mother, sitting close as if they were the dearest friends, were laying their heads together and talking both at the same time; and the horror and amazement in Mrs Bircham's face had given way to the dancing of a malicious light in her eyes, and a thrill of eagerness all over her.

'I am not at all surprised,' she was saying when Walter came in. 'I felt sure something of the kind would come to light sooner or later. I never would have trusted her – not a step beyond what I saw. I felt sure all wasn't right in that house. What a mercy, Kitty, that you saw it!'

'Wasn't it a mercy, mamma!'

Kitty gave her young husband a look aside; she had made her peace with her news. But Mrs Bircham thought of nothing – neither of her daughter's escapade, nor her own just anger – of nothing but this wonderful news, and what would be the best thing to do.

CHAPTER FIVE

'ARE WE QUITE ALONE?'

Mrs Blencarrow had just been saying goodbye to a number of her guests, and, what was of more importance, her boys had just left her upon a visit to one of their uncles who lived in a Midland county, and who, if the weather was open (and there had been a great thaw that morning), could give them better entertainment than could be provided in a feminine house. There was a look in her face as if she were almost glad to see them drive away. She was at the hall-door to see them go, and stood kissing her hand to them as they drove off shouting their goodbyes, Reginald with the reins, and Bertie with his curly head uncovered, waving his cap to his mother. She watched them till they disappeared among the trees, with a smile of pride and pleasure on her face, and then there came a dead dullness over it, like a landscape on which the sun had suddenly gone down.

'Emmy, you should not stand here in the cold,' she said; 'run upstairs, my dear, to a warm room.'

'And what are you going to do, mamma?'

'I have some business to look after,' Mrs Blencarrow said.

She went along the stone passage and down the stairs where Kitty and Walter had gone on the night of the ball. She had a weary look, and her footsteps, usually so elastic, dragged a little. The business-room was as cheerful as a large fire could make it; she opened the door with an anxious look in her eyes, but drew a breath of relief when she saw that no one was there. On the mantelpiece was a note in a large bold hand-writing: 'Out on the farm, back at five,' it said. Mrs Blencarrow sat down in the arm-chair in front of her writing-table. She leant her head in her hands, covering her face, and so remained for a long time, doing nothing, not even moving, as if she had been a figure in stone. When she stirred at last and uncovered her face, it was almost as white as marble. She drew a long sigh from the very depths of her being. 'I wonder how long this can go on,' she said, wringing her hands, speaking to herself.

These were the same words which Kitty and Walter had overheard in the dark, but not from her. There were, then, two people in the house to whom there existed something intolerable which it was wellnigh impossible to bear.

She drew some papers towards her and began to look over them listlessly, but it was clear that there was very little interest in them; then she opened a drawer and took out some letters, which she arranged in succession and tried to fix her attention to, but neither did these succeed. She rose up, pushing them impatiently away, and began to pace up and down the room, pausing mechanically now and then to look at the note on the mantelpiece and to look at her watch, both of which things she did twice over in five minutes. At five! It was not four yet – what need to linger here when there was still an hour – still a whole hour? Mrs Blencarrow was interrupted by a knock at her door; she started as if it had been a cannon fired at her ear, and instinctively cast a glance at the glass over the mantelpiece to smooth the agitation from her face before she replied. The servant had come to announce a visitor – Mrs Bircham – awaiting his mistress in the drawing-room. 'Ah! she has come to tell me about Kitty,' Mrs Blencarrow said to herself.

She went upstairs wearily enough, thinking that she had no need to be told what had become of Kitty, that she knew well enough what must have happened, but sorry, too, for the mother, and ready to say all that she could to console her – to put forth the best pleas she could for the foolish young pair. She was so full of trouble and perplexity herself, which had to be kept in rigorous concealment, that anything of which people could speak freely, upon which they could take others into their confidence, seemed light and easy to her. She went upstairs without a suspicion or alarm – weary, but calm.

Mrs Bircham did not meet her with any appeal for sympathy either in look or words; there was no anxiety in her face. Her eyes were full of satisfaction and malice, and ill-concealed but pleasurable excitement.

'I can see,' said Mrs Blencarrow, 'that you have news of Kitty,' as she shook hands with her guest.

'Oh, Kitty is right enough,' said the other hastily; and then she cast a glance round the room. 'Are we quite alone?' she asked; 'there are so many corners in this room, one never knows who may be listening. Mrs Blencarrow, I do not come to speak of Kitty, but about yourself.'

'About myself?'

'Oh,' said Mrs Bircham, with a gasp, 'you speak in that innocent tone as if it was quite surprising that anyone could have anything to say of you.'

Mrs Blencarrow changed her position so as to get her back to the light; one of those overwhelming flushes which were habitual to her had come scorching over her face.

'No more surprising to me than – to any of us,' she said, with an attempt at a smile. 'What is it that I have done?'

'Oh, Mrs Blencarrow – though why I should go on calling you Mrs Blencarrow when that's not your name –'

'Not my name!' There was a shrill sort of quaver in her voice, a keen note as of astonishment and dismay.

'I wish,' cried Mrs Bircham, growing red, and fanning herself with her muff in her excitement – 'I wish you wouldn't go on repeating what I say; it's maddening – and always as if you didn't know. Why don't you call yourself by your proper name? How can you go on deceiving everybody, and even your own poor children, living on false pretences, "lying all round," as my husband says? Oh, I know you've been doing it for years; you've got accustomed to it, I suppose; but don't you know how disgraceful it is, and what everybody will say?'

Had there been any critic of human nature present, it would have gone greatly against Mrs Blencarrow that she was not astonished at this attack. She rose up with a fine gesture of pride.

'This is an extraordinary assault to make upon me,' she said, 'in my own house.'

'Is it your own house, after disgracing it so?' cried the visitor. And then she added, after an angry pause for breath: 'I came out of kindness, to let you know that everything was discovered. Mr Bircham and I thought it was better you should have it from a friend than from common report.'

'I appreciate the kindness,' said Mrs Blencarrow, with something like a laugh; then she walked to the side of the fire and rang the bell. Mrs Bircham trembled, but her victim was perfectly calm; the assailant looked on in amazed expectation, wondering what was to come next, but the assailed stood quietly waiting till the servant appeared. When the man opened the door, his mistress said: 'Call Mrs Bircham's carriage, John, and attend her downstairs.'

Mrs Bircham stood gasping with rage and astonishment. 'Is that all?' she said; 'is that all you have got to say?'

'All – the only reply I will make,' said the lady of the house. She made her visitor a stately bow, with a wave of the hand towards the door. Mrs Bircham, half mad with baffled rage, looked round as it were for some moral missile to throw before she took her dismissal. She found it in the look of the man who stood impassive at the door. John was a well-trained servant, bound not to look surprised at anything. Mrs Bircham clasped her hands together, as if she had made a discovery, made a few hasty steps towards the door, and then turned round with an offensive laugh. 'I suppose that's the man,' she said.

Mrs Blencarrow stood firm till the door had closed and the sound of her visitor's laugh going downstairs had died away: then she sank down upon her knees in the warm fur of the hearthrug – down – down – covering her face with her hands. She lay there for some time motionless, holding herself together, feeling like something that had suddenly fallen into ruin, her walls all crumbled down, her foundations giving way.

The afternoon had grown dark, and a grey twilight filled the great windows. Nothing but the warm glow of the fire made any light in the large and luxurious room. It was so full of the comforts and brightness of life – the red light twinkling in the pretty pieces of old silver and curiosities upon the tables, catching in ruddy reflection the picture-frames and mirror, warming and softening the atmosphere which was so sheltered and still; and yet in no monastic cell or prison had there ever been a prostrate figure more like despair.

The first thing that roused her was a soft, caressing touch upon her shoulder; she raised her head to see Emmy, her delicate sixteen-year-old girl, bending over her.

'Mamma, mamma, is anything the matter?' said Emmy.

'I was very tired and chilly; I did not hear you come in, Emmy.'

'I met Mrs Bircham on the stairs; she was laughing all to herself, but when she saw me she began to cry, and said, "Poor Emmy! poor little girl! You'll feel it." But she would not tell me what it was. And then I find you, mamma, looking miserable.'

'Am I looking miserable'? You can't see me, my darling,' said her mother with a faint laugh. She added, after a pause: 'Mrs Bircham has got a new story against one of her neighbours. Don't let us pay any attention, Emmy; I never do, you know.'

'No, mamma,' said Emmy, with a quaver in her voice. She was very quiet and said very little, but in her half-invalid condition she could not help observing a great many things that eluded other people, and many alarms and doubts and suppressed suspicions were in her mind which she could not and would not have put in words. There was something in the semi-darkness and in the abandon in which she had found her mother which encouraged Emmy. She clasped Mrs Blencarrow's arm in both of hers, and put her face against her mother's dress.

'Oh, mamma,' she said, 'if you are troubled about anything, won't you tell me? Oh, mamma, tell me! I should be less unhappy if I knew.'

'Are you unhappy, Emmy? – about me?'

'Oh! I did not mean quite that; but you are unhappy sometimes, and how can I help seeing it? I know your every look, and what you mean when you put your hands together – like that, mamma.'

'Do you, Emmy?' The mother took her child into her arms with a strong pressure, as if Emmy's feeble innocence pressed against her own strong, struggling bosom did her good. The girl felt the quiver in her mother's arm, which enfolded her, and felt the heavy beating of the heart against which she was pressed, with awe and painful sympathy, but without suspicion. She knew everything without knowing anything in her boundless sympathy and love. But just then the clock upon the mantelpiece tingled out its silvery chime. Five o'clock! Mrs Blencarrow put Emmy out of her arms with a sudden start. 'I did not think it was so late. I have to see someone downstairs at five o'clock.'

'Oh, mamma, wait for some tea; it is just coming.'

'You are very late,' said Mrs Blencarrow to the butler, who came in carrying a lamp, while John followed him with the tray. Tea in the afternoon was a very novel invention, at that time known only in a few houses. 'Do not be so late another day. I must go, Emmy – it is business; but I shall be back almost directly.'

'Oh, mamma, I hate business; you say you will be back directly, and you don't come for hours!'

Mrs Blencarrow kissed her daughter and smiled at her, patting her on the shoulder.

'Business, you know, must be attended to,' she said, 'though everything else should go to the wall.'

Her face changed as she turned away; she gave a glance as she passed at the face of the man who held open the door for her, and it seemed to Mrs Blencarrow that there was a gleam of knowledge in it, a suppressed disrespect. She was aware, even while this idea framed itself in her mind, that it was a purely fantastic idea, but the profound self-consciousness in her own soul tinged everything she saw; she hurried downstairs with a sort of reluctant swiftness, a longing to escape and yet an eagerness to go.

CHAPTER SIX

'IS IT TRUE?'

A few days passed without any further incident. Mrs Blencarrow's appearance in the meantime had changed in a singular way. Her wonderful self-command was shaken; sometimes she had an air of suppressed excitement, a permanent flush under her eyes, a nervous irritation almost uncontrollable; at other moments she was perfectly pale and composed, but full of an acute consciousness of every sound. She spent a great part of her time in her business-room downstairs, going and coming on many occasions hurriedly, as if by an impulse she could not resist. This could not be hidden from those keen observers, the servants, who all kept up a watch upon her, quickened by whispers that began to reach them from without. Mrs Blencarrow, on her side, realised very well what must be going on without. She divined the swiftness with which Mrs Bircham's information would circulate through the county, and the effect it would produce. Whether it was false or true would make no difference at first. There would be the same wave of discussion, of wonder, of doubt; her whole life would be investigated to see what were the likelihoods on either side, and her recent acts and looks and words all talked over. She was a very proud woman, and her sensations were something like those of a civilised man who is tied to a stake and sees the savages dancing round him, preparing to begin the torture. She expected every moment to see the dart whirl through the air, to feel it quiver in her flesh; the waiting at the beginning, anticipating the first missile, must be, she thought, the worst of all.

She watched for the first sound of the tempest, and Emmy and the servants watched her, the one with sympathy and terror, the others with keen curiosity not unheightened by expectation. She was a good mistress, and some of them were fond of her; some of them were capable of standing by her through good and evil; but it is not in human nature not to watch with excitement the bursting of such a cloud, or to look on without a certain keen pleasure in seeing how a victim – a heroine – will comport herself in the moment of danger. It was to them as good as a play. There were some in her own house who did not believe it; there were some who had long, they said, been suspicious; but all, both those who believed it and those who did not believe it, were keen to see how she would comport herself in this terrible crisis of fate.

The days went by very slowly in this extraordinary tension of spirit; the first stroke came as such a stroke generally does – from a wholly unexpected quarter. Mrs Blencarrow was sitting one afternoon with Emmy in the drawing-room. The large room looked larger with only these two in it. Emmy, a little figure only half visible, lay in a great chair near the fire, buried in it, her small face showing like a point of whiteness amid the ruddy tones of the firelight and the crimson of the chair. Her mother was on the other side of the fire, with a screen thrown between her and the glow, scarcely betraying her existence at all, in the shade in which she sat, by any movement. The folds of her velvet dress caught the firelight and showed a little colour lying coiled about her feet; but this was all that a spectator would have seen. Emmy was busy with some fleecy white knitting, which she could go on with in the partial darkness; the faint sound of her knitting-pins was audible along with the occasional puff of flame from the fire, or falling of ashes on the hearth. There was not much conversation between them. Sometimes Emmy would ask a question: 'When are the boys coming home, mamma?' 'Perhaps today,' with a faint movement in the darkness; 'but they are going back to school on Monday,' Mrs Blencarrow said, with a tone of relief. It might have been imagined that she said 'Thank Heaven!' under her breath. Emmy felt the meaning of that tone as she felt everything, but blamed herself for thinking so, as if she were doing wrong.

'It is a strange thing to say,' said Mrs Blencarrow; 'but I almost wish they were going straight back to school, without coming home again.'

'Oh, mamma!' said Emmy, with a natural protest.

'It seems a strange thing,' said Mrs Blencarrow, 'to say –' She had paused between these two last words, and there was a slight quiver in her voice.

She had paused to listen; there was some sound in the clear air, which was once more hard with frost; it was the sound of a carriage coming up the avenue. All was so still around the house that they could hear it for a long way. Mrs Blencarrow drew a long, shivering breath.

'There's somebody coming,' said Emmy; 'can it be Rex and Bertie?'

'Most likely only somebody coming to call. Emmy!'

'What, mamma?'

'I was going to say, don't stay in the room if – if it were. But no, never mind; it was a mistake; I would rather you did stay.'

'I will do whatever you please, mamma.'

'Thank you, Emmy. If I turn to you, go. But perhaps there will be no need.'

They waited, falling into a curious silence, full of expectation; the carriage came so slowly up to the door; it jingled and jogged, so that they recognised instinctively that it must be the fly from the station.

'It will be the boys, after all,' Mrs Blencarrow said, with something between relief and annoyance. 'No,' she added, with a little impatience; 'don't run to the door to meet them. It is too cold for you; stay where you are; I can't have you exposing yourself.'

Something of the irritability of nervous expectation was in her voice, and presently the door opened, but not with the rush of the boys' return. It was opened by the butler, who came in solemnly, his white shirt shining out in the twilight of the room, and announced in his grandest tone, 'Colonel and Mr d'Eyncourt,' as two dark figures followed him into the room. Mrs Blencarrow rose to her feet with a low cry. She put her hand unconsciously upon her heart, which leaped into the wildest beating.

'You!' she said. They came forward, one following the other, into the circle of the firelight, and took her hand and kissed her with solemnity: Colonel d'Eyncourt was a tall, slim, soldierly man, the other shorter and rotund. But there was something in the gravity of their entrance which told that their errand was of no usual kind. When Emmy came forward to greet her uncles, they turned to her with a mixture of impatience and commiseration.

'Are you here, my poor child?' said one; and the other told her to run away, as they had something particular to say to her mamma.

The butler in the meantime was lighting the candles on the mantelpiece, which made a sudden blaze and brought the two gentlemen into sight.

'I am sorry I did not know you were coming,' said Mrs Blencarrow, recovering her fortitude with the sudden gleam of the light, 'or I should have sent for you to the station. Preston, bring some tea.'

'No tea for us,' said Mr d'Eyncourt; 'we have come to see you on family business, if you could give us an hour undisturbed.'

'Don't bring any tea, then, Preston,' she said with a smile, 'and don't admit anyone.' She turned and looked at Emmy, whose eyes were fixed on her. 'Go and look out for the boys, my dear.'

The two brothers exchanged glances – they were, perhaps, not men of great penetration – they considered that their sister's demeanour was one of perfect calm; and she felt as if she were being suffocated, as she waited with a smile on her face till her daughter and the butler, who was more deliberate, were gone. Then she sat down again on her low chair behind the screen, which sheltered her a little from the glare of the candles as well as the fire.

'I hope,' she said, 'it is nothing of a disagreeable kind – you both look so grave.'

'You must know what we have come to talk about, Joan.'

'Indeed I don't,' she said; 'what is it? There is something the matter. Reginald – Roger – what is it? You frighten me with your grave faces – what has happened?'

The gentlemen looked at each other again; their eyes said, 'It cannot be true.' The Colonel cleared his voice; he was the eldest, and it was upon him that the special burden lay.

'If it is true,' he said – 'you know best, Joan, whether it is true or not – if it is true, it is the most dreadful thing that has happened in our family.'

'You frighten me more and more,' said Mrs Blencarrow. 'Something about John?'

John was the black sheep of the D'Eyncourt family. Again the brothers looked at each other.

'You must be aware of the rumour that is filling the county,' said the younger brother. 'I hear there is nothing else talked of, Joan. It is about you – you, whom we have always been so proud of. Both Reginald and I have got letters. They say that you have made a disgraceful marriage; that it's been going on for years; that you've no right to your present name at all, nor to your position in this house. I cannot tell you the half of what's said. The first letter we paid no attention to, but when we heard it from half a dozen different places – Joan – nothing about John could be half so bad as a story like this about you.'

Mrs Blencarrow had risen slowly to her feet, but still was in the shade. She did not seem able to resist the impulse to stand up while she was being accused.

'So this is the reason of your sudden visit,' she said, speaking with deliberation, which might have meant either inability to speak, or the utmost contempt of the cause.

'What could we have done else?' they both cried together, apologetic for the first moment. 'We, your brothers, with such a circumstantial story,' said the Colonel.

'And your nearest friends, Joan; to nobody could it be of so much importance as to us,' said the other.

'Us!' she said; 'it is of more importance to the children.'

'My dear girl,' said the Colonel, putting his hand on her shoulder, 'I am most thankful we did not trust to letters, but came. It's enough to look at you. You must give us your authority, and we will soon make an end of these slanderers. By Jove! in the old days it would have been pistols that would have done it.'

'You can't use pistols to women,' said Mr d'Eyncourt, 'if you were the greatest fire-eater that ever was.'

They both laughed a little at this, but the soul was taken out of the laugh by the perception slowly dawning upon both that Mrs Blencarrow had said nothing, did not join either in their laugh or their thankfulness for having come, and had, indeed, slightly shrunk from her brother's hand, and still stood without asking them to sit down.

'I'm afraid you are angry with us,' said Roger d'Eyncourt, 'for having hurried here as if we believed it. But there never is any certainty in such matters. We thought it better to settle it at once – at the fountain-head.'

'Yes,' she said, but no more.

The brothers looked at each other again, this time uneasily.

'My dear Joan,' said the Colonel – but he did not know how to go on.

'The fact is,' said Mr d'Eyncourt, 'that you must give us your authority to contradict it, don't you know – to say authoritatively that there is not a shadow of truth –'

'Won't you sit down?' said Mrs Blencarrow.

'Eh? Ah! Oh yes,' said both men together. They thought for a moment that she was giving them her 'authority', as they said. The Colonel rolled an easy chair near to her. Roger d'Eyncourt stood up against the glow of the fire.

'Of course, that is all we want – your word,' said the Colonel.

She was still standing, and seemed to be towering above him where he sat in that low chair; and there was a dumb resistance in her attitude which made a strange impression upon the two men. She said, after a moment, moistening her lips painfully, 'You seem to have taken the word of other people against me easily enough.'

'Not easily; oh no! with great distress and pain. And we did not take it,' said the younger brother; 'we came at once, to hear your own –'

He stopped, and there was a dead silence. The Colonel sat

bending forward into the comparative gloom in which she stood, and Roger d'Eyncourt turned to her in an attitude of anxious attention; but she made no further reply.

'Joan, for God's sake say something! Don't you see that pride is out of the question in such circumstances? We must have a distinct contradiction. Heavens! here's someone coming, after all.'

There was a slight impatient tap at the door, and then it was opened quickly, as by someone who had no mind to be put back. They all turned towards the newcomer, the Colonel whirling his chair round with annoyance. It was Brown – Mrs Blencarrow's agent or steward. He was a tall young man with a well-developed, athletic figure, his head covered with those close curling locks which give an impression of vigour and superabundant life. He came quickly up to Mrs Blencarrow with some papers in his hand and said something to her, which, in their astonishment and excitement, the brothers did not make out. He had the slow and low enunciation of the North-country, to which their ear was not accustomed. She answered him with almost painful distinctness.

'Oh, the papers about Appleby's lease. Put them on the table, please.'

He went to the table and put them down, turned for a moment undecided, and then joined the group, which watched him with a surprised and hostile curiosity, so far as the brothers were concerned. She turned her face towards him with a fixed, imperious look.

'I forgot,' she said hurriedly; 'I think you have both seen my agent, Mr Brown.'

Roger d'Eyncourt gave an abrupt nod of recognition; the Colonel only gazed from his chair.

'I thought Mr Brown had been your steward, Joan.'

'He is my – everything that is serviceable and trustworthy,' she said.

The words seemed to vibrate in the air, so full of meaning were they, and she herself to thrill with some strong sentiment which fixed her look upon this man. He paused a little as if he intended to speak, but after a minute's uncertainty, with a rustic inclination of his head, went slowly away. Mrs Blencarrow dropped suddenly into her chair as the door closed, as if some tremendous tension had relaxed. The brothers looked wonderingly at each other again. 'That is all very well; the people you employ are in your own hands; but this is of far more consequence.'

'Joan,' said the Colonel, 'I don't know what to think. For God's sake answer one way or another! Why don't you speak? For the sake of your children, for the sake of your own honour, your credit, your family – Is it true?'

'Hush, Rex! Of course we know it isn't true. But, Joan, be reasonable, my dear; let's have your word for it, that we may face the world. Of course we know well enough that you're the last woman to dishonour Blencarrow's memory – poor old fellow! who was so fond of you – and deceive everybody.'

'You seem to have believed me capable of all that, or you would not have come here!'

'No, Joan, no – not so. Do, for God's sake, take the right view of it! Tell us simply that you are not married, and have never thought of such a thing, which I for one am sure of to begin with.'

'Perhaps,' she said, with a curious hard note of a laugh, 'they have told you, having told you so much, whom I am supposed to have married, as you say.'

Again they looked at each other. 'No one,' said the Colonel, 'has told us that.'

She laughed again. 'Then if this is all you know, and all I am accused of, to have married no one knows who, no one knows when, you must come to what conclusion you please, and make what discoveries you can. I have nothing to say.'

'Joan!' they both cried.

'You must do exactly what seems good to you,' she said, rising hastily. 'Find out what you can, say what you like – you shall not have a word from me.'

CHAPTER SEVEN

A NIGHT OF MISERY

She was gone before they could say another word, leaving them looking at each other in consternation, not knowing what to think.

For the rest of the night Mrs Blencarrow shut herself up in her own room; she would not come downstairs, not even to dinner. The boys arrived and sought their mother in the drawing-room, wondering that she did not come to meet them, but found only their uncles there, standing before the fire like two baffled conspirators. Reginald and Bertie rushed to their mother's room, and plunged into it, notwithstanding her maid's exhortation to be quiet.

'Your mamma has got a bad headache, sir.'

They were not accustomed to any régime of headaches. They burst in and found her seated in her dressing-gown over the fire.

'Is your head so bad? Are you going to stay out?' said Reginald, who had just learnt the slang of Eton.

'And there's Uncle Rex and Uncle Roger downstairs,' said Bertie.

'You must tell them I am not well enough to come down. You must take the head of the table and take care of them instead of me,' said Mrs Blencarrow.

'But what is the matter, mamma?' said Bertie. 'You do not look very bad, though you are red here.' He touched his own cheeks under his eyes, which were shining with the cold and excitement of arriving.

'Never mind, my dear. Emmy and you must do the honours of the house. I am not well enough to come downstairs. Had you good sport?'

'Oh, very good one day; but then, mamma, you know this horrid frost –'

'Yes, yes. I should not wonder if the ice on the pond would bear tomorrow,' she said with a smile. 'Now run away, dear boys, and see that your uncles have everything they want; for I can't bear much talking, you know, with my bad head.'

'Poor mamma!' they cried. Reginald felt her forehead with his cold hand, as he had seen her do, and Bertie hugged her in a somewhat rude embrace. She kissed both the glowing faces, bright with cold and fun and superabundant life. When they were gone, noisily, yet with sudden starts of recollection that they ought to be quiet, Mrs Blencarrow got up from her chair and began to walk hurriedly about the room, now and then wringing her hands.

'Even my little boys!' she said to herself, with the acutest tone of anguish. 'Even my little boys!'

For she had no headache, no weakness. Her brain was supernaturally clear, seeing everything on every side of the question. She was before a problem which it needed more than mortal power to solve. To do all her duties was impossible; which was she to fulfil and which abandon? It was not a small contradiction such as sometimes confuses a brain, but one that was fundamental, striking at the very source of life. She was not angry with her brothers, or with the others who had made this assault upon her. What were they, after all? Had they never spoken a word, the problem would still have been there, more and more difficult to solve every day.

No one disturbed her further that night; she sent word downstairs that she was going to bed, and sent even her maid away, darkening the light. But when all was still, she rose again, and, bringing out a box full of papers, began to examine and read them, burning many – a piece of work which occupied her till the household noises had all sunk into silence, and the chill of midnight was within and around the great house full of human creatures asleep. Mrs Blencarrow had all the restlessness about her of great mental trouble. After she had sat long over her papers, she thrust them from her hastily, throwing some into the fire and some into the box, which she locked with a sort of fierce energy; then rose and moved about the room, pausing to look at herself, with her feverish cheeks, in the great mirror, then throwing herself on her knees by her bedside as if to pray, then rising with a despairing movement as if that was impossible. Sometimes she murmured to herself with a low, unconscious outcry like some wounded animal – sometimes relieved herself by broken words. Her restlessness, her wretchedness, all seemed to breathe that question – the involuntary cry of humanity – 'What shall I do? What shall I do?' At length she opened her door softly and stole downstairs. There was moonlight outside, and stray rays from a window here and there made the long corridors and stairs faintly visible. One broad sweep of whiteness from a great window on the staircase crossed the dark like a vast ribbon, and across this ghostly light her figure appeared and passed, more strangely and in a more awful revelation than had all been dark. Had anyone seen her, it would have been impossible to take her for anything but a ghost.

She went down to the hall, then noiselessly along the further passage and bare stone stairs to the little business-room. All was dark and silent there, the moonlight coming in through the chinks of the closed shutters. Mrs Blencarrow stood on the threshold a moment as if she had expected to find someone there, then went in and sat down a few minutes in the dark. Her movements and her sudden pauses were alike full of the carelessness of distracted action. In the solitude and midnight darkness and silence, what could her troubled thoughts be meditating? Suddenly she moved again unseen, and came out to the door by which tenants and other applicants came for business or charity. She turned the key softly, and, opening it, stood upon the threshold. The opening from the darkness into the white world unseen was like a chill and startling transformation; the white light streamed in, opening a narrow pathway in the darkness, in the midst of which she stood, a ghost indeed – enough to have curdled the blood of any spectator. She stood for another moment between the white world without and the blackness of night and sleep within. To steal away and be lost for ever in that white still distance; to disappear and let the billows of light and space and silence swallow her up, and be seen no more. Ah! but that was not possible. The only thing possible to mortal power was a weary plodding along a weary road, that led not to vague distances, but to some village or town well-known, where the fugitive would be discovered by the daylight, by wandering wayfarers, by life which no one can escape. Even should death overtake her, and the welcome chill extinguish existence, yet still there would be found somewhere, like a fallen image, her empty shell, her mortal garment lying in the way of the first passenger. No; oh no; rather still the struggle, the contradictions, the despair –

And how could she ask God to help her? – that one appeal which is instinctive: for there was nothing she could do that would not be full of lies or of treachery, a shirking of one duty or another, the abandonment of justice, truth, and love. She turned from the world outside and closed the door; then returned again up the long stairs, and crossed once more the broad belt of moonlight from the window in the stair-case. It was like resigning all hope of outside help, turning back to the struggle that had to be fought out inch by inch on the well-known and common ground. She was chilled to the heart with the icy air of the night, and threw herself down on the hearthrug before the fire, with a forlorn longing for warmth, which is the last physical craving of all wounded and suffering things; and then she fell into a deep but broken sleep, from which she fortunately picked herself up before daylight, so as to prevent any revelation of her agitated state to the maid, who naturally suspected much, but knew, thanks to Mrs Blencarrow's miraculous self-command, scarcely anything at all.

She did not get up next morning till the brothers, infinitely perplexed and troubled, believing their sister to be mortally offended by the step they had taken, and by their adoption or partial adoption of the rumours of the neighbourhood, had gone away. They made an ineffectual attempt to see her before they left, and finally departed, sending her a note, in which Roger d'Eyncourt expressed the deep sorrow of both, and their hope that she would come in time to forgive them, and to see that only solicitude for herself and her family could have induced them to take such a step.

'I hope,' he added, 'my dear sister, that you will not misunderstand our motives when I say that we are bound in honour to contradict upon authoritative grounds this abominable rumour, since our own character may be called in question, for permitting you to retain the guardianship of the children in such circumstances. As you refuse to discuss it with us (and I understand the natural offence to your pride and modesty that seems involved), we must secure ourselves by examining the books in which the record of the marriage was said to have been found.'

Mrs Blencarrow received this note while still in bed. She read it with great apparent calm, but the great bed in which she lay quivered suddenly, all its heavy satin draperies moving as if an earthquake had moved the room. Both her maid and Emmy saw this strange movement with alarmed surprise, thinking that one of the dogs had got in, or that there had been some sinking of the foundation.

'The bed shook,' said Mrs Blencarrow, clutching with her hand at the quilt, as if for safety. 'Yes, I felt something; but the flooring is not very even, and worm-eaten at some places, you know.'

She got up immediately after, making a pretence of this to account for her recovery so soon after her brothers' departure, and appeared soon afterwards downstairs, looking very pale and exhausted, but saying she felt a little better. And the day passed as usual – quite as usual to the boys and the servants; a cheerful day enough, the children in the foreground, and a good deal of holiday noise and commotion going on. Emmy from time to time looked wistfully at her mother, but Mrs Blencarrow took no notice, save with a kiss or an especially tender word.

'I think you have got my headache, Emmy.'

'Oh, mamma, I don't mind if I can take it from you.'

The mother shook her head with a smile that went to Emmy's heart.

'I am afraid,' she said, 'no one can do that.'

In the afternoon she sent a man over to the Vicarage, with a note to the clergyman of the parish. He was a middle-aged man, but unmarried; a studious and quiet parson, little in society, though regarded with great respect in the neighbourhood; a man safe to confide in, with neither wife nor other belongings to tempt him to the betrayal of a secret entrusted to him. Perhaps this was why, in her uttermost need, Mrs Blencarrow bethought herself of Mr Germaine. She passed the rest of the day in the usual manner, not going out, establishing herself behind the screen by the drawing-room fire with some work, ready to be appealed to by the children. It was the time at which she expected visits, but there had been no caller at Blencarrow for a day or two, which was also a noticeable thing, for the neighbourhood was what is called sociable, and there had been rarely a day in which some country neighbour or other did not appear, until the last week, during which scarcely any stranger had crossed the threshold. Was it the weather which had become so cold? Was it that there were Christmas parties in most of the houses, which perhaps had not quite broken up yet? Was it –? It was a small matter, and Mrs Blencarrow was thankful beyond expression to be rid of them, to be free of the necessity for company looks and company talks – but yet –

In the evening, after dinner, when the children were all settled to a noisy round game, she went downstairs to her business-room, bidding them good night before she left, and requesting that she should not be disturbed, for her head-aches lately had made her much behind with her work, which, of course, was unusually heavy at the beginning of the year. She went away with a curious stillness about her, pausing at the door to give a last look at the happy little party, all flushed with their game. It might have been the last look she should ever have of them, from the expression in her face; and then she closed the door and went resolutely away. The servants in their regions below sounded almost as merry as the children, in the after-dinner ease; but they were far from the business-room, which was perfectly quiet and empty – a shaded lamp burning in it, the fire blazing. Mrs Blencarrow sat down at her writing-table, but, though she was so busy, did nothing. She looked at her watch with a weary sigh, then leaning her head on her hands, waited – for whom and for what, who could say?

CHAPTER EIGHT

MRS BLENCARROW'S CONFESSION

She had been there for some time when the sound of a footstep on the gravel outside made her start. It was followed by a knock at the door, which she herself opened almost before the summons. She came back to the room, immediately followed by a tall man in clerical dress. The suppressed excitement which had been in Mrs Blencarrow's aspect all the day had risen now to an extraordinary height. She was very pale, with one flaring spot on either cheek, and trembled so much that her teeth were with difficulty kept from chattering against each other. She was quite breathless when she took her seat again, once more supporting her head in her hands.

The clergyman was embarrassed, too; he clasped and unclasped his hands nervously, and remarked that the night was very cloudy and that it was cold, as if, perhaps, it had been to give her information about the weather that he came. Mr Germaine giving her his views about the night, and Mrs Blencarrow listening with her face half hidden, made the most curious picture, surrounded as it was by the bare frame-work of this out-of-the-way room. She broke in abruptly at last upon the few broken bits of information which he proceeded to give.

'Do you guess why I sent for you, Mr Germaine?'

The Vicar hesitated, and said, 'I am by no means sure.'

'Or why I receive you here in this strange place, and let you in myself, and treat you as if you were a visitor whom I did not choose to have seen?'

'I have never thought of that last case.'

'No – but it is true enough. It is not an ordinary visit I asked you to pay me.' She took her hands from her face and looked at him for a moment. 'You have heard what people are saying of me?' she said.

'Yes, but I did not believe a word. I felt sure that Kitty only meant to curry favour at home.'

She gave him a strange, sudden look, then paused with a mechanical laugh. 'You think, then,' she said, 'that there are people in my own county to whom that news would be something to conciliate; something – something to make them forgive?'

'There are people everywhere who would give much for such a story against a neighbour, Mrs Blencarrow.'

'It is sad that such a thing should be.' She stopped again, and looked at him once more. 'I am going to surprise you very much, Mr Germaine. You are not like them, so I think I am going to give you a great shock,' she said.

She had turned her face towards him as she spoke; the two red spots on her cheeks were like fire, yet her paleness was extreme; they only seemed to make this the more remarkable.

In the momentary silence the door opened suddenly, and someone came in. In the subdued light afforded by the shaded lamp it was difficult to see more than that a dark figure had entered the room, and, crossing over to the further side, sat down against the heavy curtains that covered the window. Mrs Blencarrow made the slightest movement of consciousness, not of surprise, at this interruption, which, indeed, scarcely was an interruption at all, being so instantaneous and so little remarked. She went on:

'You have known me a long time; you will form your own opinion of what I am going to tell you; I will not excuse or explain.'

'Mrs Blencarrow, I am not sure whether you have perceived that we are not alone.'

She cast a momentary glance at the newcomer, unnecessary, for she was well aware of him, and of his attitude, and every line of the dark shadow behind her. He sat bending forward, almost double, his elbows upon his knees, and his head in his hands.

'It makes no difference,' she said, with a slight impatience – 'no difference. Mr Germaine, I sent for you to tell you – that it was true.'

'What!' he cried. He had scarcely been listening, all his attention being directed with consternation, almost with stupefaction, on the appearance of the man who had come in – who sat there – who made no difference. The words did not strike him at all for the first moment, and then he started and cried in his astonishment, 'What!' as if she had struck him a blow.

Mrs Blencarrow looked at him fixedly and spoke slowly, being, indeed, forced to do so by a difficulty in enunciating the words. 'The story you have heard is – true.'

The Vicar rose from his chair in the sudden shock and horror; he looked round him like a man stupefied, taking in slowly the whole scene – the woman who was not looking at him, but was gazing straight before her, with those spots of red excitement on her cheeks; the shadow of the man in the background, with face hidden, unsurprised. Mr Germaine slowly received this astounding, inconceivable thought into his mind.

'Good God!' he cried.

'I make no – explanations – no – excuses. The fact is enough,' she said.

The fact was enough; his mind refused to receive it, yet grasped it with the force of a catastrophe. He sat down helpless, without a word to say, with a wave of his hands to express his impotence, his incapacity even to think in face of a revelation so astounding and terrible; and for a full minute there was complete silence; neither of the three moved or spoke. The calm ticking of the clock took up the tale, as if the room had been vacant – time going on indifferent to all the downfalls and shame of humanity – with now and then a crackle from the glowing fire.

She said at last, being the first, as a woman usually is, to be moved to impatience by the deadly silence, 'It was not only to tell you – but to ask, what am I to do?'

'Mrs Blencarrow – I have not a word – I – it is incredible.'

'Yes,' she said with a faint smile, 'but very true.' She repeated after another pause, 'What am I to do?'

Mr Germaine had never in his life been called upon to face such a question. His knowledge of moral problems concerned the more primitive classes of humanity alone, where action is more obvious and the difficulties less great. Nothing like this could occur in a village. He sat and gazed at the woman, who was not a mere victim of passion – a foolish woman who had taken a false step and now had to own to it – but a lady of blameless honour and reputation, proud, full of dignity, the head of a well-known family, the mother of children old enough to understand her downfall and shame, with, so far as he knew, further penalties involved of leaving them, and every habit of her life, and following the man, whoever he was, into whatsoever wilderness he might seek. The Vicar felt that all the ordinary advice which he would give in such a case was stopped upon his lips. There was no parallel between what was involved here and anything that could occur among the country folk. He sat, feeling the problem beyond him, and without a word to say.

'I must tell you more,' said Mrs Blencarrow. At her high strain of excitement she was scarcely aware that he hesitated to reply, and not at all that he was so much bewildered as to be beyond speech. She went on as if she had not paused at all. 'A thing has happened – which must often happen; how can I tell you? It has been – not happy – for either. We miscalculated – ourselves and all things. If I am wrong, I am – subject – to contradiction,' she said, suddenly stopping with a gasp as if for breath.

The shades of the drama grew darker and darker. The spectator listened with unspeakable excitement and curiosity; there was a silence which seemed to throb with suspense and pain; but the figure in the background neither moved nor spoke – a large motionless figure, doubled upon itself, the shaggy head held between the hands, the face invisible, the elbows on the knees.

'You see?' she said, with a faint movement of her hands, as though calling his attention to that silence. There was a painful flicker of a smile about her lips; perhaps her pride, perhaps her heart, desired even at this moment a protest. She went on again: 'It is – as I say; you will see how this – complicates – all that one thinks of – as duty. What am I to do?'

'Mrs Blencarrow,' said the clergyman – then stopped with a painful sense that even this name could be no longer hers, a perception which she divined, and responded to with again a faint, miserable smile – 'what can I say to you?' he burst out. 'I don't know the circumstances; what you tell me is so little. If you are married a second time –'

She made a movement of assent with her hand.

'Then, of course – it is a commonplace; what else can I say? – your duty to your husband must come first; it must come first. It is the most primitive, the most fundamental law.'

'What is that duty?' she said, almost sharply, looking up; and again there was a silence.

The clergyman laboured to speak, but what was he to say? The presence of that motionless figure in the background, had there been nothing else, would have made him dumb.

'The first thing,' he said, 'in ordinary circumstances – Heaven knows I speak in darkness – would be to own your position, at least, and set everything in its right place. Nature itself teaches,' he continued, growing bolder, 'that it is impossible to go on living in a false position, acting, if not speaking, what can be nothing but a lie.'

'It is commonplace, indeed,' she cried bitterly, 'all that: who should know it like me? But will you tell me,' she said, rising up and sitting down in her excitement, 'that it is my duty to leave my children who want me, and all the work of my life which there is no one else to do, for a useless existence, pleasing no one, needed by no one – a life without an object, or with a hopeless object – a duty I can never fulfil? To leave my trust,' she went on, coming forward to the fire, leaning upon the mantelpiece, and speaking with her face flushed and her voice raised in unconscious eloquence, 'the office I have held for so many years – my children's guardian, their steward, their caretaker – suppose even that I had not been their mother, is a woman bidden to do all that, to make herself useless, to sacrifice what she can do as well as what she is?'

She stopped, words failing her, and stood before him, a wonderful noble figure, eloquent in every movement and gesture, in the maturity and dignity of her middle age; then suddenly broke down altogether, and, hiding her face, cried out:

'Who am I, to speak so? Not young to be excused, not a fool to be forgiven; a woman ashamed – and for no end.'

'If you are married,' said the Vicar, 'it is no shame to marry. It may be inappropriate, unsuitable, it may be even regrettable; but it is not wrong. Do not at least take a morbid view.'

She raised her drooping head, and turned round quickly upon him.

'What am I to do?' she said. 'What am I to do?'

The Vicar's eyes stole, in spite of himself, to the other side of the room. The dark shadow there had not moved; the man still sat with his head bent between his hands. He gave no evidence that he had heard a word of the discussion; he put forth no claim except by his presence there.

'What can I say?' said Mr Germaine. 'Nothing but commonplace, nothing but what I have already said. Before everything it is your duty to put things on a right foundation; you cannot go on like this. It must be painful to do, but it is the only way.'

'It is seldom,' she said, 'very seldom that you are so precise.'

'Because,' he said firmly, 'there is no doubt on the subject. It is as clear as noonday; there is but one thing to do.'

Mrs Blencarrow said nothing; she stood with a still resistance in her look – a woman whom nothing could overcome, broken down by circumstances, by trouble, ready to grasp at any expedient; yet unsubdued, and unconvinced that she could not struggle against fate.

'I can say nothing else,' the Vicar repeated, 'for there is nothing else to say; and perhaps you would prefer that I should go. I can be of no comfort to you, for there is nothing that can be done till this is done – not from my point of view. I can only urge this upon you; I can say nothing different.'

Again Mrs Blencarrow made no reply. She stood so near him that he could see the heaving of strong passion in all her frame, restrained by her power of self-command, yet beyond that power to conceal. Perhaps she could not speak more; at least, she did not. Mr Germaine sat between the two, both silent, absorbed in this all-engrossing question, till he could bear it no longer. He rose abruptly to his feet.

'May God give you the power to do right!' he said; 'I can say no more.'

Mrs Blencarrow followed him to the door. She opened it for him, and stood outside on the threshold in the moonlight to see him go.

'At least,' she said, 'you will keep my secret; I may trust you with that.'

'I will say nothing,' he replied, 'except to yourself; but think of what I have said.'

'Think! If thinking would do any good!'

She gave him her hand, in all the veins of which the blood was coursing like a strong stream, and then she closed the door behind him and locked it. During all this time the man within had never stirred. Would he move? Would he speak? Or could he speak and move? When she went back –

CHAPTER NINE

'I AM HER HUSBAND'

A night and a day passed after this without any incident. What the chief persons in this strange drama were doing or thinking was hid under an impenetrable veil to all the world. Life at Blencarrow went on as usual. The frost was now keen and the pond was bearing; the youngsters had forgotten everything except the delight of the ice. Even Emmy had been dragged out, and showed a little colour in her pale cheeks, and a flush of pleasure in her eyes, as she made timid essays in the art of skating, under the auspices of her brothers. When she proved too timid for much progress, they put her in a chair and drew her carriage from end to end of the pond, growing more and more rosy and bright. Mrs Blencarrow herself came down in the afternoon to see them at their play, and since the pond at Blencarrow was famed, there was a wonderful gathering of people whom Reginald and Bertie had invited, or who were used to come as soon as it was known that the pond 'was bearing.'

When the lady of the house came on to this cheerful scene, everybody hurried to do her homage. The scandal had not taken root, or else they meant to show her that her neighbours would not turn against her. Perhaps the cessation of visits had been but an accident, such as sometimes happens in those wintry days when nobody cares to leave home; or perhaps public opinion, after the first shock of hearing the report against her, had come suddenly round again, as it sometimes does, with an impulse of indignant disbelief. However that might be, she received a triumphant welcome from everybody. To be sure, it was upon her own ground. People said to each other that Mrs Blencarrow was not looking very strong, but exceedingly handsome and interesting; her dark velvet and furs suited her; her eyes were wonderfully clear, almost like the eyes of a child, and exceptionally brilliant; her colour went and came. She spoke little, but she was very gracious and made the most charming picture, everybody said, with her children about her: Emmy, rosy with unusual excitement and exercise, clinging to her arm, the boys making circles round her.

'Mamma, come on the chair – we will take you to the end of the pond.'

'Put mamma on the chair,' they shouted, laying hold upon her.

She allowed herself to be persuaded, and they flew along, pushing her before them, their animated, glowing faces full of delight, showing over her shoulders.

'Brown, come and give us a hand with mamma. Brown, just lay hold at this side. Brown! Where's Brown? Can't he hear?' the boys cried.

'Never mind Brown,' said Mrs Blencarrow; 'I like my boys best.'

'Ah! but he is such a fellow,' they exclaimed. ' He could take you over like lightning. He is far the best skater on the ice. Turn mamma round, Rex, and let her see Brown.'

'No, my darlings, take me back to the bank; I am getting a little giddy,' she said.

But, as they obeyed her, they did not fail to point out the gyrations of Brown, who was certainly, as they said, the best skater on the ice. Mrs Blencarrow saw him very well – she did not lose the sight – sweeping in wonderful circles about the pond, admired by everybody. He was heavy in repose, but he was a picture of agile strength and knowledge there.

And so the afternoon passed, all calm, bright, tranquil, and, according to every appearance, happy, as it had been for years. A more charming scene could scarcely be, even summer not brighter – the glowing faces lit up with health and that invigorating chill which suits the hardy North; the red sunset making all the heavens glow in emulation; the graceful, flying movements of so many lively figures; the boyish shouts and laughter in the clear air; the animation of everything. Weakness or trouble do not come out into such places; there was nothing but pleasure, health, innocent enjoyment, natural satisfaction there. Quite a little crowd stood watching Brown, the steward, as he flew along, making every kind of circle and figure; as if he had been on wings – far the best skater of all, as the boys said. He was still there in the ruddy twilight, when the visitors who had that privilege had streamed into the warm hall for tea, and the nimble skaters had disappeared.

The hall was almost as lively as the pond had been, the red

firelight throwing a sort of enchantment over all, rising and falling in fitful flames. Blencarrow had not been so brilliant since the night of the ball. Several of the young Birchams were there, though not their mother; and Mrs Blencarrow had specially, and with a smile of meaning, inquired for Kitty in the hearing of everybody. They all understood her smile, and the inquiry added a thrill of excitement to the delights of the afternoon.

'The horrid little thing! How could she invent such a story?' people said to each other; though there were some who whispered in corners that Mrs Blencarrow was wise, if she could keep it up, to 'brazen it out'.

Brazen it out! A woman so dignified, so proud, so self-possessed; a princess in her way, a queen-mother. As the afternoon went on, her strength failed a little; she began to breathe more quickly, to change colour instantaneously from red to pale. Anxiety crept into the clear, too clear eyes. She looked about her by turns with a searching look, as if expecting someone to appear and change everything. When the visitors' carriages came to take them away, the sound of the wheels startled her.

'I thought it might be your uncles coming back,' she said to Emmy, who always watched her with wistful eyes.

Mr Germaine had gone back to his parsonage through the moonlight with a more troubled mind than he had perhaps ever brought before from any house in his parish. A clergy-man has to hear many strange stories, but this, which was in the course of being enacted, and at a crisis so full of excitement, occupied him as no tale of erring husband or wife, or son or daughter going to the bad – such as are also so common everywhere – had ever done. But the thing which excited him most was the recollection of the silent figure behind, sitting bowed down while the penitent made her confession, listening to everything, but making no sign. The clergyman's interest was all with Mrs Blencarrow; he was on her side. To think that she – such a woman – could have got herself into a position like that, seemed incredible, and he felt with an aching sympathy that there was nothing he would not do to get her free – nothing that was not contrary to truth and honour. But, granted that inconceivable first step, her position was one which could be understood; whereas all his efforts could not make him understand the position of the other – the man who sat there and made no sign. How could any man sit and hear all that and make no sign? – silent when she made the tragical suggestion that she might be contradicted – motionless when she herself did the servant's part and opened the door to the visitor – giving neither support, nor protest, nor service – taking no share in the whole matter except the silent assertion of his presence there? Mr Germaine could not forget it; it pre-occupied him more than the image, so much more beautiful and commanding, of the woman in her anguish. What the man could be thinking, what could be his motives, how he could reconcile himself to, or how he could have been brought into, such a strange position, was the subject of all his thoughts. It kept coming uppermost all day; it became a kind of fascination upon him; wherever he turned his eyes he seemed to see the strange image of that dark figure, with hidden face and shaggy hair pushed about, between his supporting hands.

Just twenty-four hours after that extraordinary interview these thoughts were interrupted by a visitor.

'A gentleman, sir, wishing to see you.'

It was late for any such visit, but a clergyman is used to being appealed to at all seasons. The visitor came in – a tall man wrapped in a large coat, with the collar up to his ears. It was a cold night, which accounted sufficiently for any amount of covering. Mr Germaine looked at him in surprise, with a curious sort of recognition of the heavy outline of the man; but he suddenly brightened as he recognised the stranger and welcomed him cheerfully.

'Oh! it is you, Brown; come to the fire, and take a chair. Did you ever feel such cold?'

Brown sat down, throwing back his coat and revealing his dark countenance, which was cloudy, but handsome, in a rustic, heavy way. The frost was wet and melting on his crisp, curly brown beard; he had the freshness of the cold on his face, but yet was darkly pale, as was his nature. He made but little response to the Vicar's cheerful greeting, and drew his chair a little distance away from the blaze of the fire. Mr Germaine tried to draw him into conversation on ordinary topics, but finding this fail, said, after a pause:

'You have brought me, perhaps, a message from Mrs Blencarrow?'

He was disturbed by a sort of presentiment, an uneasy feeling of something coming, for which he could find no cause.

'No, I have brought no message. I come to you,' said Brown, leaning forward with his elbows on his knees, and his head supported by his hands, 'on my own account.'

Mr Germaine uttered a strange cry.

'Good heavens!' he said, 'it was you!'

'Last night?' said Brown, looking up at him with his deep-set eyes. 'Didn't you know?'

Mr Germaine could not contain himself. He got up and pushed back his chair. He looked for a moment, being a tall man also and strong, though not so strong as the Hercules before him, as if he would have seized upon him and shaken him, as one dog does another.

'You!' he cried. 'The creature of her bounty! For whom she has done everything! Obliged to her for all you are and all you have!'

Brown laughed a low, satirical laugh. 'I am her husband,' he said.

The Vicar stood with rage in his face, gazing at this man, feeling that he could have torn him limb from limb.

'How dared you!' he said, through his clenched teeth; 'how dared you? I should like to kill you. You to sit there and let her appeal to you, and let her open to me and close the door, and do a servant's office, while you were there!'

'What do you mean?' said Brown. 'I am her husband. She told you so. It's the woman's place in my class to do all that; why shouldn't she?'

'I thought,' said the Vicar, 'that however much a man stood by his class, it was thought best to behave like a gentleman, whatever you were.'

'There you were mistaken,' said Brown. He got up and stood beside Mr Germaine on the hearth, a tall and powerful figure. 'I am not a gentleman,' he said, 'but I've married a lady. What have I made by it? At first I was a fool. I was pleased whatever she did. But that sort of thing don't last. I've never been anything but Brown the steward, while she was the lady and mistress. How is a man to stand that? I've been hidden out of sight. She's never acknowledged me, never given me my proper place. Brought up to supper at the ball by those two brats of boys, spoken to in a gracious sort of way, "My good Brown." And I her husband – her husband, whom it was her business to obey!'

'It is a difficult position,' said Mr Germaine, averting his eyes.

'Difficult! I should think it was difficult, and a false position, as you said. You spoke to her like a man last night; I'm glad she got it hot for once. By –! I am sick and tired of it all.'

'I hope,' said the Vicar, not looking at him, 'that you will not make any sudden exposure, that you will get her consent, that you will respect her feelings. I don't say that you have not a hard part to play; but you must think what this exposure will be for her.'

'Exposure!' he said. 'I can't see what shame there is in being my wife; naturally I can't see it. But you need not trouble your head about that. I don't mean to expose her. I am sick and tired of it all; I'm going off to begin life anew –'

'You are going off?' Mr Germaine's heart bounded with sudden relief; he could scarcely believe the man meant what he said.

'Yes, I'm going off – to Australia. You can go and tell her. Part of the rents have been paid in this week; I have taken them for my expenses.'

He took out a pocket-book, and held it out to the Vicar, who started and laid a sudden hand on his arm.

'You will not do that – not take money?' he cried. 'No, no, that cannot be!'

'Why not? You may be sure she won't betray me. I am going for her good and my own; I don't make any pretence; it's been a failure all round. I want a wife of my own age and my own kind, not a grand lady who is disgusted with all my natural ways. A man can't stand that,' he cried, growing darkly red. 'She kept it under at first. But I am not a brute, whatever you think. I have done all I can for her, to save her from what you call the exposure, and I take this money fairly and above-board; you can tell her of it. I wouldn't have chosen even you for a confidant if she hadn't begun. You can go and tell her I sail for Australia from Liverpool tomorrow, and shall never see her more.'

'Brown,' said the Vicar, still with his hand on the other's arm, 'I don't know that I can let you go.'

'You'll be a great fool, then,' Brown said.

The two men stood looking at each other, the one with a smile, half of contempt, half of resolution, the other troubled and uncertain. 'They will say you have gone off with the money – absconded.'

'She'll take care of that.'

'Brown, are you sure she wishes you to go? The exposure will come, all the same; everything is found out that is true; and she will be left to bear it alone without any support.'

'There will be no exposure,' he said with a short laugh; 'I've seen to that, though you think me no gentleman. There's no need for another word, Mr Germaine; I've a great respect for you, but I'm not a man that is to be turned from his purpose. You can come and see me off if you please, and make quite sure. I'm due at the station in an hour to catch the up-train. Will you come? – and then you can set her mind quite at ease and say you have seen me go.'

Mr Germaine looked at his comfortable fire, his cosy room, his book, though he had not been reading, and then at the cold road, the dreary changes of the train, the sleepless night. After a time he said, 'I'll take your offer, Brown. I'll go with you and see you off.'

'If you like, you can give me into custody on the way for going off with Mrs Blencarrow's money. Mrs Blencarrow's money? not even that!' he cried, with a laugh of bitterness. 'She is Mrs Brown; and the money's the boy's, not hers, or else it would be lawfully mine.'

'Brown,' said the Vicar tremulously, 'you are doing a sort of generous act – God help us! – which I can't help consenting to, though it's utterly wrong; but you speak as if you had not a scrap of feeling for her or anyone.'

'I haven't!' he cried fiercely, 'after three years of it. Half the time and more she's been ashamed of me, disgusted with me. Do you think a man can stand that? By –! I neither can nor will. I'm going,' he continued, buttoning his coat hastily; 'you can come or not, as you please.'

'You had better have some supper first,' said the Vicar.

'Ah! that's the most sensible word you have said,' cried Brown.

Was it bravado, was it bitterness, was it relief in escaping, or the lightness of despair? Mr Germaine could never tell. It was something of all of these feelings, mingled with the fierce pride of a peasant slighted, and a certain indignant contemptuous generosity to let her go free – the woman who was ashamed of him. All these were in Brown's thoughts.

CHAPTER TEN

'HE HAS GONE — FOR EVER!'

Mrs Blencarrow spent that evening with her children; she made no attempt to leave them after dinner. A lull had come into her heart after the storm. She was aware that it was only temporary, nothing real in it; but in the midst of a tempest even a few minutes of stillness and tranquility are dear. She had found on the mantelpiece of the business-room the intimation, 'Away on business till Monday,' and though it perplexed, it also soothed her. And the brothers returning with the proof of Kitty's statement, the extract which no doubt they would bring from those books to confound her, could now scarcely arrive tonight. A whole evening undisturbed among the children, who might so soon be torn from her, in her own familiar place, which might so soon be hers no longer; an evening like the past, perhaps the last before the coming of that awful future when she must go forth to frame her life anew, loveless and hopeless and ashamed. It was nothing but 'the torrent's smoothness ere it dash below,' the moment of calm before the storm; and yet it was calm, and she was thankful for that one soft moment before the last blow fell.

The children were again lively and happy over their round game; the sober, kind governess – about whom Mrs Blencarrow had already concluded in her own mind that she could secure at least the happiness of the little ones if their mother were forced to leave them – was seated with them, even enjoying the fun, as it is a blessed dispensation of Providence that such good souls often do. Emmy was the only one who was out of it; she was in her favourite corner with a book, and always a watchful glance at her mother. Emmy, with that instinct of the heart which stood her in place of knowledge, had a perception, she could not have told how, of the pause in her mother's soul. She would do nothing to disturb that pause. She sat praying mutely that it might last, that it might be peace coming back. Naturally Emmy, even with all her instinct, did not know the terrible barrier that stood between her mother and peace.

And thus they all sat, apparently in full enjoyment of the sweet household quiet, which by moments was so noisy and full of commotion, the mother seated with the screen between her and the great blazing fire, the children round the table, Emmy with her book.

Mrs Blencarrow's eyes dwelt upon them with the tenderest, the most pathetic of smiles.

> She looked on sea, and hill, and shore,
> As she might never see them more,

with a throb of tragic wonder rising in her heart how she could ever have thought that this was not enough for her – her children, and her home, and this perfect peace.

It was already late and near their bedtime when the fly from the station drove up to the door. Mrs Blencarrow did not hear until some minutes after Emmy had raised her head to listen, and then for a moment longer she would not hear it, persuading herself that it was the wind rising among the trees. When at last it was unmistakable, and the great hall-door was heard to open, and even – or so she thought in the sudden shiver of agitation that seized her – a breath of icy wind came in, sweeping through the house, she was for the moment paralyzed with dismay and fear. She said something to hurry the children to bed, to bid them go – go! But she was inaudible even to herself, and did not attempt, nor could indeed form any further thought on any subject, except horror of the catastrophe which she felt to be approaching in this moment of peace. If it had but waited till tomorrow! Till an hour later, when she should have been alone!

Motionless, holding by her chair, not even hearing the wondering question, 'Who can be coming so late?' Mrs Blencarrow, with wide-open eyes fixed on the door, and her under-lip dropping in mortal anguish, awaited her fate.

It was the avengers returning from their search; her brothers hurrying in one after the other. The Colonel said, 'How delightfully warm!' rubbing his hands. Roger (Roger was always the kindest) came up to her and took her hand. She had risen up to meet them, and grasped with her other hand the only thing she could find to support her – the top of the screen which stood between her and the fire.

'Joan!' her brothers began, both speaking together.

She was hoarse; her lips were baked, it was all she could do to articulate.

'Nothing before the children!' she said, with a harsh and breathless voice.

'Joan, this does not matter. We have come to beg your pardon, most humbly, most penitently.'

'Fact is, it must all have been a mistake –'

'Say an invention, Reginald.'

'An invention – a cursed lie of that confounded girl! Hallo!'

There was a sudden crash and fall. The children all rushed to see, and Mrs Blencarrow stood with the light streaming upon her, and the gilt bar of the screen in her hand. She had crushed it in her agitated grasp; the pretty framework of gilded wood and embroidery lay in a heap at her feet. The sound and shock had brought the blood rushing to her ghastly tragical countenance. She stood looking vaguely at the bar in her hand; but none of the children had any eyes for her – they were all on their knees in a group round the gilded ruin. Save Mr d'Eyncourt and Emmy, no one noticed the terrible look in her face.

'Come and sit down here while they pick up the pieces,' said Roger. 'Joan, I am afraid you are very angry, and you have reason; that we should have believed such a slander – of all the women in the world – of you! But, my dear, we are heartily ashamed of ourselves, if that is anything.'

'Most penitent,' said the Colonel, 'thoroughly ashamed. I said to Roger, "If ever there were men who had reason to be proud of their sister –"'

'And yet we gave a moment's credence to such a barefaced lie!'

She heard them dimly as from a far distance, and saw them as through a fog; but the voices thus echoing and supplementing each other like a dull chorus gave her time to recover. She said sedately, not with any enthusiasm:

'I am glad that you have found out your mistake.'

Oh, heaven! Oh, miserable fate! But it was no mistake.

Mrs Blencarrow found herself after a time taking Kitty's defence.

'She got her own pardon for it. Her mother is a great gossip, and loves a tale against her neighbour. Don't blame the girl too much.'

'If you excuse her, Joan, who should say a word? But why in all the world, thinking of an unlikely person to fasten such a slander upon, did she choose you?'

'Am I so unlikely, when my brothers believed it?' she said, with a strange smile.

An hour full of commotion followed. The boys never tired in showing each other and everybody else the flaw in the wood where the framework of the screen had broken.

'But you must have leant on it very heavily, mamma.'

'She wanted to break our heads with it,' said the Colonel, who was in high spirits.

'Fancy mamma breaking Uncle Rex's head with the screen!' the children cried with shrieks of laughter; and thus, in a tumult of amusement and gaiety, the evening closed.

Mrs Blencarrow went to her room with something cold and hard at her heart like a stone. They had begged her pardon. They had not found that record. By some chance, by some miracle – how could she tell what? – she had escaped detection. But it was true; nothing could alter the fact. Nothing could spirit away *him* – the husband – the man to whom she had bound herself; the owner of her allegiance, of herself, if he chose to exercise his rights. It occurred to her, in the silence of her room, when she was alone there and dared to think, that her present escape was but an additional despair. Had they found it, as they ought to have found it, the worst would have been over. But now, to have the catastrophe indefinitely postponed – to have it before her every day – the sword hanging over her head, her mind rehearsing day and night what it would be! Would it not be better to go and tell them yet, to have it over? Her hand was on her door to obey this impulse, but her heart failed her. Who could tell? God might be so merciful as to let her die before it was known.

The two gentlemen spent a very merry morning on the ice with the children, and in the afternoon left Blencarrow the best of friends with their sister, grateful to her for her forgiveness. Mrs Blencarrow did not think it necessary to go out to the pond that afternoon – she was tired, she said – and the skating, which often lasts so short a time that everybody feels it a duty to take advantage of it, had cleared the house. She spent the afternoon alone, sitting over the fire, cold with misery and anxiety and trouble. Everything seemed right again, and yet nothing was right – nothing. False impressions, false blame, can be resisted; but who can hold up their head against a scandal that is true?

It was one of the women servants, in the absence of everybody else, who showed Mr Germaine into the drawing-room. He was himself very cold and fatigued, having travelled all the previous night, and half the day, returning home. He came to the fire and stood beside her, holding out his hands to the warmth.

'You are alone, Mrs Blencarrow?'

'Quite alone. You look as if you had something to tell me. For God's sake what is it? No news can come to me but bad news,' she said, rising, standing by him, holding out her hands in piteous appeal.

'I don't know whether you will think it bad news or good. I have come straight from Liverpool, from the deck of a ship which sailed for Australia today.'

'What do you mean? What do you mean? A ship – which sailed for Australia?'

'I have come from – Everard Brown. He has thought it best to go away. I have brought you a statement of all the affairs, showing how he has carried with him a certain sum of money. Mrs Blencarrow, it is too great a shock; let me call someone.'

'No!' She caught at his arm, evidently not knowing what it was upon which she leant. 'No, tell me all – all!'

'He has taken means – I know not what – to destroy all evidence. He has gone away, never meaning to return. It is all wrong – wrong from beginning to end, the money and everything; but he had a generous meaning. He wanted to set you free. He has gone – for ever, Mrs Blencarrow!'

She had fallen at his feet without a word.

People said afterwards that they had thought for some time that Mrs Blencarrow was not looking well, that she was in a state to take any illness. And there was a flaw in the drains which nobody had discovered till then. She had a long illness, and at one time was despaired of. Things were complicated very much by the fact that Brown, her trusted and confidential agent, had just emigrated to Australia, a thing he had long set his heart upon, before she fell ill. But her brother, Mr Roger d'Eyncourt, was happily able to come to Blencarrow and look after everything, and she recovered, finally, being a woman with a fine constitution and in the prime of life. The family went abroad as soon as she was well enough to travel, and have remained so, with intervals in London, ever since. When Reginald comes of age, Blencarrow will no doubt be opened once more; but the care of the estate had evidently become too much for his mother, and it is not thought that she will venture upon such a charge again. It is now in the hands of a regular man of business, which is perhaps better on the whole.

Kitty fell into great and well-deserved disgrace when it was found out that she had seen what nobody else could see. Walter even, with a man's faculty for abandoning his partner in guilt, declared that he never saw it, that Kitty must have dreamt it, that she tried to make him believe it was Joan Blencarrow when it was only Jane Robinson, and many other people were of the opinion that it was all Kitty's cleverness to get herself forgiven and her own runaway match condoned.

That match turned out, like most others, neither perfect happiness nor misery. Perhaps neither husband nor wife could have explained ten years after how it was that they were so idiotic as to think that they could not live without each other; but they get on together very comfortably, all the same.

QUEEN ELEANOR
AND FAIR ROSAMOND

CHAPTER ONE

THE FAMILY

Mr and Mrs Lycett-Landon were two middle-aged people in the fulness of life and prosperity. Though they belonged to the world of commerce, they were both well-born and well-connected, which was not so common, perhaps, thirty years ago as it is now. He was the son of an Irish baronet; she was the daughter of a Scotch laird. He had never, perhaps, been the dashing young man suggested by his parentage, though he rode better than a business man has any call to ride, and had liked in moderation all his life the pleasures which business men generally can only afford themselves when they have grown very rich. Mr Lycett-Landon was not very rich in the Liverpool sense of the word, and he had never been very poor. He had accepted his destination in the counting-house of a distant relation, who was the first to connect the name of Landon with business, without any heartbreak or abandonment of brighter dreams. It had seemed to him from the beginning a sensible and becoming thing to do. The idea of becoming rich had afforded him a rational satis-faction. He had not envied his brothers their fox-hunting, their adventures in various parts of the world, their campaigning and colonising. Liverpool, indeed, was prosaic but very comfortable. He liked the comfort, the sensation of always having an easy balance at his bankers (bliss, indeed! and like every other kind of bliss, so out of reach to most of us), the everyday enjoyment of luxury and well-being, and was indifferent to the prosaic side of the matter. His marriage was in every sense of the word a good marriage; one which filled both families with satisfaction. She had money enough to help him in his business, and business connections in the West of Scotland (where the finest people have business connections), which helped him still more; and she was a good woman, full of accomplishments and good-humour and intelligence. In those days, perhaps, ladies cultivated accomplishments more than they do now. They did not give themselves up to music or to art with absorbing devotion, becoming semi- or more than semi-professional, but rather with a general sense that to do lovely things was their vocation in the world, pursued the graces tenderly all round, becoming perhaps excellent in some special branch because it was more congenial than the others, but no more. Thus while Mrs Lycett-Landon was far from equal to Mozart and Beethoven, and would have looked on Bach with alarm, and Brahms with consternation, in dance music, which her children demanded incessantly, she had no superior. The young people preferred her to any band. Her time was perfect, her spirit and fire contagious – nothing under five-and-twenty could keep still when she played, and not many above. And she was an admirable mistress of a house, which is the first of all the fine arts for a woman. What she might have been as a poor man's wife, with small means to make the best of, it is unnecessary to inquire, for this was fortunately not her role in life. With plenty of money and of servants, and a pretty house and everything that was necessary to keep it up, she was the most excellent manager in the world. Perhaps now and then she was a trifle hard upon other women who were not so well off as she, and saw the defects in their management, and believed that in their place she would have done better. But this is a fault that the most angelic might fall into, and which only becomes more natural and urgent the more benevolent the critic is, till sometimes she can scarcely keep her hands from meddling, so anxious is she to set the other right. It was to Mrs Lycett-Landon's credit, as it is to that of many like her, that she never meddled; though while she was silent, her heart burned to think how much better she would have done it. Her husband was somewhat of the same way of thinking in respect to men in business who did not get on. He said, 'Now, if So-and-so would only see –' while his wife in her heart would so fain have taken the house out of the limp hands of Mrs So-and-so and set everything right. It is a triumph of civilisation, and at the same time a great trial to benevolent and clear-sighted people, that according to the usages of society the So-and-so's must always be left to muddle along in their own way.

Lycett, Landon, Fareham & Co (Mr Lycett-Landon combined the names and succession of two former partners) had houses in Liverpool, Glasgow, and London, and a large business. I think they were cotton-brokers, without having any very clear idea what that means. But this will probably be quite unimportant to the reader. The Lycett-Landons had begun by living in one of the best parts of Liverpool, which in those days had not extended into luxurious suburbs as now, or at least had done so in a very much lesser degree; and when the children came, and it was thought expedient to live in the country, they established themselves on the other side of the Mersey, in a great house surrounded by handsome gardens and grounds overlooking the great river, which, slave of commerce as it is and was, was then a very noble sight, as no doubt it continues to be. To look out upon it in the darkening, or after night had fallen, to the line of lights opposite, when the darkness hid everything that was unlovely in the composition of the great town and its fringe of docks, and to watch the great ships lying in midstream with lights at their masts and bows, and the small sprites of attendant steamboats, each carrying its little lamp, as they rustled to and fro, threading their way among the anchored giants, crossing and recrossing at a dozen different points, was an endless pleasure. I do not speak of the morning, of the sunshine, shining tranquil upon the majestic stream, flashing back from its miles of waters, glowing on the white spars and sails, the marvellous aerial cordage, the great ships resting from their labours, each one of them a picture, because that is a more common sight. But there are, or were, few things so grand, so varied, so full of interest and amusement, as the Mersey at night. There were times, indeed, when it was very cold, and rarer times when it was actually dangerous to cross the ferry; when the world was lost in a white fog, and a collision was possible at every moment. But these exciting occasions were few, and in ordinary cases the Lycett-Landons, great and small, thought the crossing a pleasant adjunct both to the business and pleasure which took them to vulgar Liverpool. Vulgar was the name they were fond of applying to it, with that sense of superiority which is almost inevitable in the circumstances, in people conscious of living out of it, and of making of it a point of view, a feature in the landscape. But yet there was a certain affection mingled with this contempt. They rather liked to talk of the innumerable masts, the miles of docks, and when their visitors fell into enthusiasm with the scene, felt both pleasure and pride as in an excellence which they had themselves some credit from – 'A poor thing, sir, but mine own'; and they felt a little scorn of those who did not see how fine the Mersey was with its many ships, although they affected to despise it in their own persons. These were the affectations of the young. Mr Lycett-Landon himself had a solid satisfaction in Liverpool. He put all objections down at once with statistics and an intimation that people who did not respect the second seaport in the kingdom were themselves but little worthy of respect. His wife, however, was like the young people, and patronised the town.

At the time when the following incidents began to happen the family consisted of six children. These happy people had not been without their griefs, and there was more than one gap in the family. Horace was not the eldest, nor was little Julian the youngest of the children. But these times of grief had passed over, as they do, though no one can believe it, and scarcely disturbed the general history of happiness looking

back upon it, though they added many experiences, made sad
thoughts familiar, and gave to the mother at least a sanctuary
of sorrow to which she retired often in the bustle of life, and
was more strengthened than saddened, though she herself
scarcely knew this. Horace was twenty, and his sister Millicent
eighteen, the others descending by degrees to the age of six.
There was a great deal of education going on in the family,
into which Mrs Lycett-Landon threw herself with fervour,
only regretting that she had not time to get up classics with
the boys, and with great enthusiasm throwing herself into the
music, the reading, all the forms of culture with which she had
already a certain acquaintance. These pursuits filled up the
days which had already seemed very fully occupied, and there
were moments when papa, coming home after his business,
declared that he felt himself quite 'out of it', and lingered in
the dining-room after dinner and dozed instead of coming
upstairs. But there is nothing more common than that a man
of fifty, a comfortable merchant, after a very comfortable
dinner, should take a little nap over his wine, and nobody
thought anything of it. Horace was destined for business, to
take up the inheritance of his father, which was far too considerable to be let fall into other hands; and though the young
man had his dreams like most young men, and now and then
had gratified himself with the notion that he was making
a sacrifice, for the sake of his family, of his highest aspirations,
yet in reality he was by no means dissatisfied with his destination, and contemplated the likelihood of becoming a very
rich man, and raising the firm into the highest regions of
commercial enterprise, with pleasure and a sense of power

which is always agreeable. Naturally, he thought that his father and old Fareham were a great deal too cautious, and did not make half enough of their opportunities; and that when 'new blood', meaning himself, came in, the greatness and the rank of merchant princes, to which they had never attained, would await the house. He had been a little shy at first to talk of this, feeling that ambition of a commercial kind was not heroic, and that his mother and Milly would be apt to gibe. But what ambition of an aspiring youth was ever gibed at by mother and sister? They found it a great and noble ambition when they discovered it. Milly's cheeks glowed and her eyes shone with the thought. She talked of old Venice, whose merchants were indeed princes, generals, and states-men, all in one. There are a great many fine things ready existing to be said on this subject, and she made the fullest use of them. The father was rich and prosperous, and able to indulge in any luxury; but Horace should be great. A great merchant is as great as any other winner of heroic successes. Thus the young man was encouraged in his aspirations. Mr Lycett-Landon did not quite take the same view. 'He'll do very well if he keeps up to what has been done before him,' he said. 'Don't put nonsense into his head. Yes; all that flummery about merchant princes and so forth is nonsense. If he goes to London with that idea in his head, there's no telling what mischief he may do.'

'My dear,' said Mrs Lycett-Landon, 'it must always be well to have a high aim.'

'A high fiddlestick!' said the father; 'if he does as well as I have done, he'll do very well.' And this sentiment was perhaps natural, too; for though there are indeed parents who rejoice in seeing their sons surpass them, there are many on the other side who, feeling their own work extremely meritorious, entertain natural sentiments of derision for the brags of the inexperienced boy who is going to do so much better. 'Wait till he is as old as I am,' Mr Lycett-Landon said.

'So long as he is not swept away into society,' said the mother. 'Of course, when he is known to be in town, he will be taken a great deal of notice of, and asked out –'

'Oh, to Windsor Castle, I daresay,' said papa, and laughed.

He was in one of his offensive moods, Milly said. It was very seldom he was offensive, but there are moments when a man must be so, against the united forces of youth and maternal sympathy with youth, in self-defence. Unless he means to let them have it all their own way he must be disagreeable from time to time. Mr Lycett-Landon asserted himself very seldom, but still he had to do it now and then; and though there was nothing in the world (except Milly) that he was more proud of than Horace, called him a young puppy, and wanted to know what anybody saw in him that he was to do so much better than his father. But the ladies, though they resented it for the moment, knew that there was not very much in this.

It was to the London house that Horace was destined. He was to spend a year in it 'looking about him', picking up an acquaintance with the London variety of mercantile life, learning all the minutiæ of business, and so forth. At present it was under the charge of a distant relative of Mr Fareham's, who, as soon as Horace should be able to go alone in the paths of duty, was destined to a very important post in the American house, which at present was small, but which Fareham's cousin was to make a great deal of. In the meantime, Mr Lycett-Landon himself paid frequent visits to town to see that all was going well, and would sometimes stay there for a fortnight, or even three weeks, much jested at by his wife and daughter when he returned.

'Papa finds he can do a great deal of business at the club,' said Milly; 'he meets so many people, you know. The London cotton-brokers go to all the theatres, and to the Row in the morning. It is so much nicer than at Liverpool.'

'You monkey!' her father said with a laugh. He took it very good-humouredly for a long time. But a joke that is carried on too long gets disagreeable at the last, and after a while he became impatient. 'There, that's enough of it,' he would say, which at first was a little surprising, for Milly used, so far as papa was concerned, to have everything her own way.

CHAPTER TWO

THE LONDON OFFICE

'Again – so soon!'

This is what Mrs Lycett-Landon and Milly said in chorus as the head of the house, with something which might have been a little embarrassment, announced a third visit to London in the course of four months. There was an absence of his usual assured tone – a sort of apologetic accent, which neither of them identified, but which both were vaguely conscious of, as expressing something new.

'Robert,' said his wife, 'you are anxious about young Fareham; I feel sure of it. Things are not going as you like.'

'Well, my dear, I didn't want to say anything about it, and you must not breathe a syllable of this to Fareham, who would be much distressed; but I am a little anxious about the young fellow. Discipline is very slack at the office. He goes and comes when he likes, not like a man of business. In short, I want to keep an eye upon him.'

'Oh, papa,' cried Milly, 'what a dear you are! and I that have been making fun of you about the club and the Row!'

'Never mind, my dear,' said her father, magnanimously;

'your fun doesn't hurt. But now that you have surprised my little secret, you must take care of it. Not a word, not a hint, not so much as a look, to any of the Farehams. I would not have it known for the world. But, of course, we must not expose Horace to the risk of acquiring unbusiness-like habits.'

'Oh, and most likely fast ways,' cried Mrs Lycett-Landon, 'for they seldom stop at unbusiness-like habits.' She had grown a little pale with fright. 'Oh, not for the world, Robert – our boy, who has never given us a moment's anxiety. I would rather go to London myself, or to the end of the world.'

'Fortunately, that's not necessary,' he said with a smile, 'and you must not jump at the worst, as women are so fond of doing. I have no reason to suppose he is fast, only a little disorderly, and not exact as a business man should be – he wants watching a little. For goodness sake, not a word to Fareham of all this. I would not for any consideration have him know.'

'Don't you think perhaps he might have a good influence? He has been so kind to his nephew.'

'That is just the very thing,' said Mr Lycett-Landon. 'He has been very kind (young Fareham is not his nephew, by the way, only a distant cousin), and, naturally, he would take a tone of authority, or preach, or take the after-all-I've-done-for-you tone, which would never do. No, a little watching – just the sense that there is an eye on him. He has a great many good qualities,' said the head of the house with a little pomp of manner; 'and I think – I really think – with a little care, that we'll pull him through.'

'Papa, you are an old dear,' said Milly with enthusiasm. Perhaps he did not like the familiarity of the address, or the rush she made at him to give him a kiss. At least, he put her aside somewhat hastily.

'There, there,' he said, 'that will do. I have got a great many things to look after. Have my things packed, my dear, and send them over to Lime Street Station to meet me. You can put in some light clothes, in case the weather should change. One never knows what turn it may take at this time of the year.'

It was April, and the weather had been gloomy; it was quite likely it might change, as he said, though it was not so easy to tell what he could want with his grey suit in town. This, however, the ladies thought nothing of at the moment, being full of young Fareham and his sudden declension from the paths of duty. 'And he was always so steady and so well-behaved,' cried Mrs Lycett-Landon. She saw after her husband's packing, which was a habit she had retained from the old days, when they were not nearly so rich. 'He was always a model young man; that was why I was so pleased to think of him as a companion for Horace.'

'These model young men are just the ones that go wrong,' said Milly, with that air of wisdom which is so diverting to older intelligences. Her mother laughed.

'Of course your experience is great,' she said; 'but I don't think that I am of that opinion. If a boy is steady till he is five-and-twenty, he is not very likely to break out after. Perhaps your father's prejudice in favour of business habits –'

'Mamma! It was you who said a young man seldom stopped there.'

'Was it? Well, perhaps it was,' said Mrs Lycett-Landon, with a little confusion. 'I spoke without thought. One should not be too hard on young men. They can't all be made in the same mould. Your father was always so exact, never missing the boat once – and he cannot bear people who miss the boat; so, I hope, perhaps it is not so bad as he thinks.'

'It would-never do,' said Milly, still with that air of solemnity, 'to have Horace thrown in the way of anyone who is not quite good and right.'

At this her mother laughed, and said, 'I am afraid he must be put out of the world then, Milly. I hope he has principles of his own.'

Notwithstanding this sudden levity, Mrs Lycett-Landon fully agreed – later in the day, when the portmanteau had gone to the Lime Street Station, and she and her daughter had followed it and seen papa off by the train – that it was very important Horace should make his beginning in business under a prudent and careful guide; and that if there was any irregularity in young Fareham, it was very good of papa to take so much pains to put it right. Horace, who went home with them, was but partially let into the secret, lest, perhaps, he might be less careful than they were, and let some hint drop in the office as to the object of his father's journey. The ladies questioned him covertly, as ladies have a way of doing. What did the office think of young Mr Fareham in London? Was he liked? Was he thought to be a good man of business? What did Mr Pearce say, who was the head clerk and a great authority?

'I say,' said Horace, 'why do you ask so many questions

about Dick Fareham? Does he want to marry Milly? Well, it looks like it, for you never took such notice of him before.'

'To marry me!' said Milly, in a blaze of indignation. 'I hope he is not quite so idiotic as that.'

'He is not idiotic at all; he is a very nice fellow. You will be very well off if you get any one half as good.'

'I think,' said the mother, 'that papa and I will make all the necessary investigations when it comes to marrying Milly. Now make haste, children, or we shall miss the first boat.'

It was an April evening, still light and bright, though the air was shrewish, and the wind had some east in it, blighting the gardens and keeping the earth grey, but doing much less harm to the water, which was all ruffled into edges of white. The ten minutes' crossing was not enough to make these white crests anything but pleasant, and the big ships lay serenely in mid-stream, owning the force of the spring breeze by a universal strain at their anchors, but otherwise with a fine indifference to all its petty efforts. The little ferry steam-boat coasted along big sides with much rustle and commotion, churning up innocent waves. It was quite a considerable little party of friends and neighbours who crossed habitually in this particular boat, for the Lycett-Landons lived a little way up the river – not in bustling Birkenhead. They were all so used to this going and coming, and to constant meetings during this little voyage, that it was like a perpetually recurring water-party – a moment of holiday after the work of the day. The ladies had been shopping, the men had all escaped from their offices; they had the very last piece of news, and carried with them the evening papers, the new 'Punch' – everything that was new. If there was any little cloud upon the family after their parting with papa, it blew completely away in the fresh wind; but there was not, in reality, any cloud upon them, nor any cause for anxiety or trouble. Even the mother had no thought of anything of the kind, no anticipation that was not pleasant. Life had gone so well with her that, except when one of the children was ailing, she had no fear.

Mr Lycett-Landon on this occasion was a long time in London. He did not return till nearly the end of May, and he came back in a very fretful, uncomfortable state of mind. He told his wife that he was more uneasy than ever; he did not blame young Fareham; he did not know whether it was he that was to be blamed; but things were going wrong somehow. 'Perhaps it is only that he doesn't know how to keep up discipline,' he said, 'and that the real fault is with the clerks. I begin to doubt if it's safe to leave a lot of young fellows together. It will be far safer to keep Horace here under my own eye, and with old Fareham, who is exactitude itself. He will do a great deal better. I don't think I shall send him to London.'

'Of course, Robert, I should prefer to keep him at home,' she said, 'but I am afraid after all that has been said it will disappoint the boy.'

'Oh, disappoint the boy! What does it matter about disappointing them at that age? They have plenty of time to work it out. It is at my time of life that disappointment tells.'

'That is true, no doubt,' said the mother; 'but we are used to disappointment, and they are not.'

He turned upon her almost savagely. 'You! What disappointments have you ever had?' he cried, with such an air of contemptuous impatience as filled her with dismay.

'Oh, Robert!' She looked at him with eyes that filled with tears. 'Disappointment is too easy a word,' she said.

'You mean the – the children. What a way you women have of raking up the departed at every turn. I don't believe, in my view of the word, you ever had a disappointment in your life. You never desired anything very much and had it snatched from you just when you thought –' He stopped suddenly. 'How odd,' he said, with a strange laugh, 'that I should be discussing these sort of things with you!'

'What sort of things? I can't tell you how much you astonish me, Robert. Did you ever desire anything so very much and I not know?'

Then he turned away with a shrug of his shoulders. 'You are so matter of fact. You take everything *au pied de la lettre*,' he said.

This conversation remained in Mrs Lycett-Landon's mind in spite of her efforts to represent to herself that it was only a way of speaking he had fallen into, and could mean nothing. How could it mean anything except business, or the good of the children, or some other perfectly legitimate desire? But yet, in none of these ways had he any disappointment to endure. The children were all well and vigorous, and, thank God, doing as well as heart could desire. Horace was as good a boy as ever was; and business was doing well. There was no failure, so far as she was aware, in any of her husband's hopes. It must be an exaggerated way of speaking. He must have allowed the disorder in the London office to get on his nerves; and he had the pallid, restless look of a man in suspense. He could not keep quiet. He was impatient for his letters, and dissatisfied when he had got them. He was irritable with the children, and even with herself, stopping her when she tried to consult him about anything. 'What is it?' or 'About those brats again?' he said, peevishly. This was when she wanted his opinion about a governess for little Fanny and Julian.

'What between Milly's balls and Fanny's governess you drive me distracted. Can't you settle these trifles yourself when you see how much occupied I am with more important things?'

'I never knew before that you thought anything more important than the children's welfare,' she said.

'If there was any real question of the children's welfare,' he answered, with more than equal sharpness.

It came almost to a quarrel between them. Mrs Lycett-Landon could not keep her indignation to herself. 'Because the London office is not in good order!' she could not help saying to Milly.

'Oh! mamma, dear, something more than that must be bothering him,' the girl said, and cried.

'I fear that we shall have to leave our nice home and settle in London. It is like a monomania. I believe your father thinks of nothing else night and day.'

Mrs Lycett-Landon said this as if it were something very terrible; but, perhaps, it was scarcely to be expected that Milly would take it in the same way. 'Settle in London!' she said; and a gleam of light came into her eyes. The father came into the room at the end of this consultation and heard these words.

'Who talks of settling in London?' he said.

'My dear Robert, it seems to me it must come to that; for if you are so uneasy about the office, and always thinking of it –'

'I suppose,' he said, 'it is part of your nature to take everything in that matter-of-fact way. I am annoyed about the London office; but rather than move you out of this house I would see the London office go to the dogs any day. I don't mind,' he added, with a little vehemence, 'the coming and going; but to break up this house, to transplant you to London, there is nothing in the world I would not sooner do.'

She was a little surprised by his earnestness. 'I am very glad you feel as I do on that point. We have all been so happy here. But I, for my part, would give up anything to make you more satisfied, my dear.'

'That is the last thing in the world to make me satisfied. Whatever happens, I don't want to sacrifice you,' he said, in a subdued tone.

'It would not be a sacrifice at all; what fun it would be: and then Horry need never leave us,' cried Milly. 'For my part, I should like it very much, papa.'

'Don't let us hear another word of such nonsense,' he said, angrily; and his face was so dark and his tone so sharp that Miss Milly did not find another word to say.

CHAPTER THREE

ALARMS

It was rather a relief to them all when the father went away again. They did not say so indeed in so many words, still keeping up the amiable domestic fiction that the house was not at all like itself when papa was away. But as a matter of fact there could be little doubt that the atmosphere was clear after he was gone. A certain sulphurous sense of something volcanic in the air, the alarm of a possible explosion, or at least of the heat and mutterings that precede storms, departed with him. He himself looked brighter when he went away. He was even gay as he waved his hand to them from the railway carriage, for they had gone very dutifully to see him off, as was the family custom. 'Papa is quite delighted to get off to his beloved London,' Milly said. 'He feels that things go well when he is there,' her mother replied, feeling a certain need to be explanatory. The household life was all the freer when he was gone. The young people had a great many engagements, and Mrs Lycett-Landon was very pleasantly occupied with these and with her younger children, and with all the manifold affairs of a large and full house. As happens so often, though the fundamental laws were not infringed, there was yet a little enlarging, a little loosening of bonds when the head of the house was not there. Mamma never objected to be 'put out' for any summer pleasure that might arise. She did not mind changing the dinner-hour, or even dispensing with dinner altogether, to suit a country expedition, a garden-party, or a picnic, which was a thing impossible when papa's comfort was the first thing to be thought of. It was June, and life was full of such pleasures to the young people. Horace, indeed, would go dutifully to the office every morning, endeavouring to emulate the virtue of his father, and never miss the nine o'clock boat; though as this high effort cost him in most cases his breakfast, his mother was much perplexed on the subject, and not at all sure that such goodness did not cost more than it was worth. But he very often managed to be back for lunch, and the amusements for the afternoon were endless. Mr Lycett-Landon wrote very cheerfully when he got back to London: he told his wife that he thought he saw his way to establishing matters on a much better footing, and that, after all, Dick Fareham was not at all a bad fellow; but he would not send Horace there for some time, till everything was in perfect order, and in the meantime felt that his own eye and supervision were indispensable. 'I shall hope by next year to get everything into working order,' he said. The family were quite satisfied by these explanations. There was noth-ing impassioned in their affection for their father, and Mrs Lycett-Landon was happy with her children, and quite satisfied that her husband should do what he thought best. So long as he was well, and pleasing himself, she was not at all exacting. Marriage is a tie which is curiously elastic when youth is over and the reign of the sober everyday has come in. There is no such union, and yet there is no union that sits so lightly. People who are each other's only confidants, and cannot live without each other, yet feel a half-relief and sense of emancipation when accidentally and temporarily they are free of each other. A woman says to her daughter, 'We will do so-and-so and so-and-so when your father is away,' meaning no abatement of loyalty or love, but yet an unconscious, unaccustomed, not unenjoyable freedom. And the man no doubt feels it perhaps more warmly on his side. So it was not felt that there was anything to be uncomfortable about, or even to regret. The letters were not so frequent as the wife could have wished. She sent a detailed history of the family, and of everything that was going on, every second day; but her husband's replies were short, and there were much longer intervals between. Sometimes a week would elapse without any news; but so much was going on at home, and all minds were so fully occupied, that no particular notice was taken. Mrs Lycett-Landon asked, 'How is it that you are so lazy about writing?' and there was an end of it. So long as he was perfectly well, as he said he was, what other danger could there be to fear?

There are times when the smallest matter awakens family anxiety, and there are other times when people are un-accountably, inconceivably easy in their minds, and will not take alarm whatever indications of peril may arise. When real calamity is impending how often is this the case! Ears that are usually on the alert are deafened; eyes that look out the most eagerly, lose their power of vision. Little Julian had a whitlow on his finger, and his mother was quite unhappy about it; but as for her husband, she was at rest and feared nothing. When he wrote, after a long silence, that he felt one of his colds coming on and was going to nurse himself, then indeed she felt a momentary uneasiness. But his colds were never of a dangerous kind; they were colds that yielded at once to treatment. She wrote immediately, and bade him be sure and stay indoors for a day or two, and sent him Dr Moller's prescription, which always did him good. 'If you want me, of course you know I will come directly,' she wrote. To this letter he replied much more quickly than usual, begging her on no account to disturb herself, as he was getting rapidly well again. But after this there was a longer pause in the correspondence than had ever happened before.

On one of these evenings she met her husband's partner, old Fareham, as he was always called, at dinner, at a large sumptuous Liverpool party. There was to be a great ball that evening, and Mrs Lycett-Landon and her two eldest children had come 'across' for the two entertainments, and were to stay all night. The luxury of the food and the splendour of the accompaniments I may leave to the imagination. It was such a dinner as is rarely to be seen out of commercial circles. The table groaned, not under good cheer, as used to be the case, but under silver of the highest workmanship, and the most costly flowers. The flowers alone cost as much as would have fed a street full of poor people, for they were not, I need scarcely say, common ones, things that any poor curate or even clerk might have on his table, but waxy and wealthy exotics, combinations of the chemist's skill with the gardener's, all the more difficult to be had in such profusion because the season was summer and the gardens full of Nature's easy production. Mr Fareham nodded to his partner's wife, catching her eye with difficulty between the piles of flowers. 'Heard from London lately?' he said across the table, and nodded again several times when she answered, 'Not for some days.' Old Fareham was usually a jocose old gentleman, less perfect in his manners than the other member of the firm, and of much lower origin, though perhaps more congenial to the atmosphere in which he lived; but he was not at all jocose that evening. He had a cloud upon his face. When his genial host tried to rouse him to his usual 'form' (for what can be more disappointing than an amusing man who will not do anything to amuse?) he would brighten up for a moment, and then relapse into dullness. As soon as he came into the drawing-room after dinner he made his way to his partner's wife.

'So you haven't been hearing regularly from London?' he said, taking up his post in front of her, and bending over her low chair.

'I didn't say that; I said not for a few days.'

'Neither have we,' said old Fareham, shaking his white head. 'Not at all regular. D'ye think he is quite well? He has been a deal in town this year.'

She could scarcely restrain a little indignation, thinking if old Fareham only knew the reason, and how it was to save his relative and set him right! But she answered in an easy tone, 'Yes, he has thought it expedient – for various reasons.' If he had the least idea of his nephew's irregularities, this, she thought, would make him wince.

But it did not. 'Oh, for various reasons?' he said, lifting his shaggy eyebrows. 'And did you think it expedient too?'

'You know I enter very little into business matters,' she replied, with the calm she felt. 'Of course we all miss him very much when he is away from home; but I never have put myself in Robert's way.'

'You've been a very good wife to him,' said the old man with a slight shake of the head, 'an excellent wife; and you don't feel the least uneasy? Quite comfortable about his health, and all that sort of thing? I think I'd look him up if I were you.'

'Have you heard anything about his health? Is Robert ill, Mr Fareham, and you are trying to break it to me?' she said, springing to her feet.

'No, no, nothing of the sort,' he said, putting his hand on her arm to make her reseat herself. 'Nothing of the sort; not a word! I know no more than you do – probably not half or quarter so much. No, no, my dear lady, not a word.'

'Then why should you frighten me so?' she said, sitting down again with a flutter at her heart, but a faint smile; 'you gave me a great fright. I thought you must have heard something that had been concealed from me.'

'Not at all, not at all,' said the old man. 'I'm very glad you're not uneasy. Still it is a bad practice when they get to stay so long from home. I'd look him up if I were you.'

'Do you know anything I don't know?' she said, with a recurrence of her first fear.

'No, no!' he cried – 'nothing, nothing, I know nothing; but I don't think Landon should be so long absent. That's all; I'd look him up if I were you.'

Mrs Lycett-Landon did not enjoy the ball that night. For some time indeed she hesitated about going. But Milly and Horace were much startled by this idea, and assailed her with questions – What had she heard? Was papa ill? Had anything happened? She was obliged to confess that nothing had happened, that she had heard nothing, but that old Fareham thought papa should not be so long away, and had asked if she were not uneasy about his health. What if he should be ill and concealing it from them? The children paled a little, then burst forth almost with laughter. Papa conceal it from them! he who always wanted so much taking care of when he was poorly. And why should he conceal it? This was quite unanswerable; for to be sure there was no reason in the world why he should not let his wife know, who would have gone to him at once, without an hour's delay. So they went to the ball, and spent the night in Liverpool, and next morning remembered nothing save that old Fareham was always disagreeable. 'If he knew your father's real object in spending so much time in London!' Mrs Lycett-Landon said. It was her husband's generous wish to keep this anxiety from the old man; and how little such generous motives are appreciated in this world. It was evening before they returned home – for of course with so large a family there is always shopping to do, and the ladies waited till Horace left the office. But when they reached The Elms, as their house was called, there was a letter waiting which was not comfortable. It was directed in a hand which they could scarcely identify as papa's; not from his club as usual, nor on the office paper – with no date but London. And this was what it said:

> My DEAR, – You must not be disappointed if I write only a few words. I have hurt my hand, which makes writing uncomfortable. It is not of the least importance, and you need not be uneasy: but accept the explanation if it should happen to be some days before you hear from me again. Love to the children.
> – Yours affectionately,   R L L

Mrs Lycett-Landon grew pale as she read this note. 'I see it all,' she said; 'there has been an accident, and Mr Fareham did not like to tell me of it. Horace, where is the book of the trains? I must go at once. Run, Milly, and put up a few things for me in my travelling-bag.'

'What is it, mother? Hurt his hand? Oh, but that is not much,' Horace said.

'It is not much perhaps; but to be so careful lest I should be anxious is not papa's way. "If it should happen to be some days –" Why, it is ten days since he wrote last. I am very anxious. Horry, my dear, don't talk to me, but go and see about the trains at once.'

'I know very well about the trains,' said Horace. 'There is one at ten, but then it arrives in the middle of the night. Stop at all events till tomorrow morning. I will telegraph.'

'I am going by that ten train,' his mother said.

'Which arrives between three and four in the morning!'

'Never mind, I can go to the Euston, where papa always goes. Perhaps I shall find him there. He has never said where he was living.'

'You may be sure,' said Horace, 'you will not find him at the Euston. No doubt he is in the old place in Jermyn Street. He only goes to the Euston when he is up for a day or two.'

'I shall find him easily enough,' Mrs Lycett-Landon said.

And then a little bustle and commotion ensued. Dinner was had which nobody could eat, though they all said it was probably nothing, and that papa would laugh when he knew the disturbance his letter had made. At least the children said this, their mother making little reply. Milly thought he would be much surprised to see mamma arrive in the early morning. He would like it, Milly thought. Papa was always disposed to find his own ailments very important, and thought it natural to make a fuss about them. She wanted to accompany her mother, but consented, not without a sense of dignity, that it was more necessary she should stay at home to look after the children and the house. But Horace insisted that he must go; and though Mrs Lycett-Landon had a strange disinclination to this which she herself could not understand, it seemed on the whole so right and natural that she could not stand out against it. 'There is no occasion,' she said. 'I can look after myself quite well, and your father too.' But Horace refused to hear reason, and Milly inquired what was the good of having a grown-up son if you did not make any use of him? Their minds were so free, that they both tittered a little at this, the title of grown-up son being unfamiliar and half absurd, in Milly's intention at least. She walked down with them to the boat in the soft summer night. The world was all aglow with softened lights – the moon in the sky, the lamps on the opposite bank, reflecting themselves in long lines in the still water, and every dim vessel in the roadway throwing up its little sea-star of colour. 'I shouldn't wonder,' said Milly, 'if it is a touch of the gout, like that he had last year, and no accident at all.'

'So much the more need for good nursing,' her mother said, as she stepped into the boat.

Milly walked back again with Charley, her next brother, who was fifteen. They went up to the summer-house among the trees and watched the boat as it went rustling, bustling through the groups of shipping in the river, and made little bets between themselves as to whether it would beat the Birkenhead boat, or if the Seacombe would get there first of all. There were not so many ferry-boats as usual at this hour of the night, but one or two were returning both up and down the river which had been out with pleasure-parties, with music sounding softly on the water. 'It is only that horrid old fiddle if we were near it,' said Milly, 'but it sounds quite melodious here' – for the soft night and the summer air, and the influence of the great water, made everything mellow. The doors and windows of the happy house were still all open. It was full of sleeping children and comfortable servants, and life and peace, though the master and the mistress were both away.

CHAPTER FOUR

GOING TO LOOK HIM UP

They reached London in the dawn of the morning, when the blue day was coming in over the housetops, before the ordinary stir of the waking world had begun. Of course, at that early hour it was impossible to do anything save to take refuge in the big hotel, and try to rest a little till it should be time for further proceedings. They found at once from the sleepy waiter who received them that Mr Lycett-Landon was not there. He remembered the gentleman; but they hadn't seen him not since last summer, the man said.

'I told you so, mamma,' said Horace; 'he is in Jermyn Street, of course. If he had been anywhere else, he would have put the address.'

They drove together to Jermyn Street as soon as it was practicable, but he was not there; and the landlord of the house returned the same answer that the waiter at the Euston had done. Not since last summer, he said. He had been wondering in his own mind what had become of Mr Lycett-Landon, and asking himself if the rooms or the cooking had not given satisfaction. It was a thing that had never happened to him with any of his gentlemen, but he had been wondering, he allowed, if there was anything. He would have been pleased to make any alteration had he but known. Mrs Lycett-Landon and her son looked at each other somewhat blankly as they turned away from this door. She smiled and said, 'It is rather funny that we should have to hunt your father in this way. One would think his movements would be well enough known. But I suppose it's this horrid London.' She was a little angry and hurt at the horrid London which takes no particular note even of a merchant of high standing. In Liverpool he could not have been lost sight of, and even here it was ridiculous, a thing scarcely to be put up with.

'Oh, we'll soon find him at the club,' Horace said; and they drove there accordingly, more indignant than anxious. It was still early, and the club servants had scarcely taken the trouble to wake up as yet. Club porters are not fond of giving addresses, knowing how uncertain it is whether a gentleman may wish to be pursued to their last stronghold. The porter in the present instance hesitated much. He said Mr Lycett-Landon had not been there for some time; that there was a heap of letters for him, which he took out of a pigeon-hole and turned over in his hands as he spoke, and among which Horace (with a jump of his heart) thought he could see some of his mother's; but nothing had been said about forwarding them, and he really couldn't take upon himself to say that he knowed the address.

'But I'm his son,' said Horace.

The porter looked at him very knowingly. 'That don't make me none the wiser, sir,' he said with great reason.

The youth went out to his mother somewhat aghast. 'They

don't know anything of him here,' he said; 'they say he hasn't been for long. There's quite a pile of letters for him.'

'Then we must go to the office,' Mrs Lycett-Landon said. 'He must have been very busy, or – or something.'

That was an assertion which no one could dispute. When the cab drove off again she repeated the former speech with an angry laugh. 'It *is* ridiculous, Horace, that you and I should have to run about like this from pillar to post, as if papa could slip out of sight like a – like a – mere clerk.' The mercantile world does not make much account of clerks, and she did not feel that she could find anything stronger to say.

'Nobody would believe it,' said Horace, 'if we were to tell them; but in the City it will be different,' he added, gravely.

In Liverpool it must be allowed the City was not thought very much of. It had not the same prestige as the great mercantile town of the north. The merchant princes were considered to belong to the seaports, and the magnates of the City had an odour of city feasts and vulgarity about them; but in the present circumstances it had other attractions.

'The name of Lycett-Landon can't be unknown there,' said the lad.

His mother was wounded even by this assertion. She drew herself up. 'A Lycett-Landon has no right to be unknown anywhere,' she said. 'We don't need to take our importance from any firm, I hope. But London is insufferable; nobody is anybody that comes from what they are pleased to call the country "here."'

There was an indignant tone in Mrs Lycett-Landon's voice. But yet she too felt, though she would not acknowledge it, that for once the City would be the most congenial. They drove along through the crowded, noisy streets in a hansom, feeling, after all, a little more at home among people who were evidently going to business as the men did in their own town. The sight of a well-brushed, well-washed, gold-chained commercial magnate in a white waistcoat with a rose in his button-hole did them good. And thus they arrived at 'the office', that one home-like spot amid all the desert of unaccustomed streets.

'Perhaps,' the mother said, 'we shall find him here, ready to laugh at us for this ridiculous expedition.'

'Well, I hope not,' said Horace, 'for he will be angry. Papa doesn't like to be looked after.'

This speech chilled Mrs Lycett-Landon a little, for it was quite true; and for her part she was not a woman who liked to be found fault with on account of silly curiosity. As a matter of fact, few women do. So that it was with a little check to their eagerness that they got out at the office door among all the press of people coming to their daily labour. Horace, though he had been intended to work there, scarcely knew the place; and his mother, though she had driven down three or four times to pick up her husband on the occasions when they were in town together, was but little better acquainted with it. And the clerks did not at all recognise these very unlikely visitors. Ladies appeared very seldom at the office, and at this early hour never.

'Your father, of course, would not be here so early,' Mrs Lycett-Landon said as they went upstairs; 'and I don't suppose young Mr Fareham either is the sort of person – but we must ask for Mr Fareham.'

Remembering all that her husband had said, she did not in the least expect to find that young representative of the house. How curious it was to wait until she had been inspected by the clerk, to be asked who she was, to be requested to take a seat, till it was known if Mr Fareham was disengaged! An impulse which she could scarcely explain restrained her from giving her name, which would at once have gained her all the respect she could have desired; and for the first time in her life Mrs Lycett-Landon realised what it must be to come as a poor petitioner to such a place. The clerks made their observations on her and her son behind their glass screen. They decided that she must want a place in the office for the young fellow, but that Fareham would soon give her her answer. These young men did not think much of the personal appearance of Horace, who was clearly from the country – a lanky youth whom it would be difficult to make anything of. Their consternation was extreme when young Mr Fareham, coming out somewhat superciliously to see who wanted him, exclaimed suddenly, 'Mrs Landon!' and went forward holding out his hands. 'If I had known it was you!' he said. 'I hope I have not kept you waiting. But some mistake must have been made, for I was not told your name.'

'It was no mistake,' she said, looking graciously at the young clerk, who stood by very nervous and abashed. 'I did not give my name. We shall not detain you a moment, we only want an address.'

While she spoke she had time to remark the perfectly correct and orthodox appearance of young Fareham, of whom it was almost impossible to believe that he had ever committed an irregularity of any description in the course of his life. He led the way into his room with all the respect which was due to the wife of the chief partner, and gave her a chair. 'My time is entirely at your service,' he said; 'too glad to be able to be of any use.'

Mrs Lycett-Landon sat down, and then there ensued a moment of such embarrassment as perhaps in all her life she had never known before. There was a certain surprise in the air with which he regarded her, and not the slightest appearance of any idea what she could possibly want him for at this time in the morning. And somehow this surprised unconsciousness on his part brought the most curious painful consciousness to her. She was silent; she looked at him with a kind of blank appeal. She half rose again to go away without putting her question. She seemed to be on the eve of a betrayal, of a family exposure. How foolish it was! She looked at Horace's easy-minded, tranquil countenance, and took courage.

'Do you expect,' she said, 'Mr Landon here today?' with a smile, yet a catch of her breath.

'Mr Landon!' The astonishment of young Fareham was extreme. 'Is he in town? We have not seen him since May.'

'Horace,' said Mrs Lycett-Landon, half-rising from her chair and then falling back upon it. 'Horace, your father must be very ill. He must have had – some operation – he must have thought I would be over-anxious –'

She became very pale as she uttered these broken words, and looked as if she were going to faint; and Horace, too, stared with bewildered eyes. Young Fareham began to be alarmed. He saw that his quick response was altogether unexpected, and that there was evidently some mystery.

'Let me see,' he said, appearing to ponder, 'perhaps I am making a mistake. Yes, I am sure he was here in May – he had just come back from the Continent. Wasn't it so? Oh, then, I must have misunderstood him. I thought he said – now I remember, he certainly was here in town. Yes, came to tell me something about letters – what was it?'

'Perhaps where you were to send his letters,' Mrs Landon said quickly. 'That is what we want to know.' While she was listening to him, her mind had been going through a great many questions, and she had brought herself summarily back to calm. If it should be serious illness, all her strength would be wanted. She must not waste her forces with foolish fainting or giving in, but husband them all.

Then there arose an inquiry in the office. One clerk after another was called in to be questioned. One said Mr Lycett-Landon's letters were all forwarded to the Liverpool house, or to The Elms, Rockferry, his private address; another, that they were sent to the club; and it was not till some time had been lost that one of the youngest remembered an address to which he had once been sent, to a lodging where Mr Landon was staying. He remembered all about it, for it was a pretty house, with a garden, very unlike Jermyn Street.

'It was just after Mr Landon came back from abroad,' the youth said; and by degrees he remembered exactly where it was, and brought it written down, in a neat, clerkly hand, on an office envelope. It was a flowery address, a villa in a road, both of them fanciful with a cockney sentiment.

Mrs Lycett-Landon took the paper from him with a smile of thanks; but she was so bewildered and confused that she rose up and went out of the office without even saying good-morning to young Fareham.

'Mamma, mamma,' cried Horace after her, 'you have never said –'

'Oh, don't trouble her,' said young Fareham; 'I can see she is anxious. You'll come back, won't you, and let me know if you've found him? But I hope there is some mistake.'

He did not say what kind of mistake he hoped for, nor did Horace say anything as he followed his mother. He, like Milly, thought it impossible that papa would have hidden himself thus to be ill. He was a little nervous of speaking to his mother when he saw how pale and preoccupied she looked.

'Shall I call a cab?' he said. 'Mother, do you really think there is so much to fear?'

'He has never been on the Continent,' was all his mother could say.

'No; that's true. They just have got that into their heads. It was no business of theirs where he went.'

'It is everybody's business where a man goes – a man like him. I think I know what it is, Horace. He has been fretful for some time, and restless; he must have been ill, and he has been going through an operation. Don't say anything; I feel sure of it. Perhaps there was danger in it, and he feared the fuss, and that I should be over-anxious.'

'We always thought as children that papa liked to be made a fuss with,' said simple Horace.

'You thought so in the nursery, because you liked it your-selves. Yes, we had better have a cab. How full the streets are! one cannot hear oneself talking.'

Then she was silent a little till the hansom was called. It was a very noisy part of the City, where the traffic is continual, and it was very difficult to hear a woman's voice. She paused before she got into the cab.

'Now I think of it,' she said, 'you had better go and tele-graph to Milly, for she will be anxious. Go back to the hotel and do it. Tell her that we have got to town all safe, and that you will send her word this evening how papa is.'

'But, mother, you are not going without me! and it will be better to telegraph after we know.'

'That is what I wish you to do, Horace. It might upset him. I think it a great deal better for me to go by myself. Just do what I tell you. Milly will want to know that we have arrived all right; and wait at the hotel till I send for you.'

'You had much better let me come with you, mother.'

The noise was so great that she only made a 'No' with her mouth, shaking her head as she got into the cab, and gave him the address to show the cabman. Then, before Horace had awakened from his surprise, she was gone, and he was left feeling very solitary, pushed about by all the passers-by upon the pavement. The youth was half angry, half astonished. To go back to the hotel was not a thing that tempted him, but he was so young that he obeyed by instinct, meaning to pour forth his indignation to Milly. Even in a telegram there is a possibility of easing one's heart.

CHAPTER FIVE

THE HOUSE WITH THE
FLOWERY NAME

Mrs Lycett-Landon drove off through the crowded City streets
in a curious trace of excited feeling. She had a sense that
something was going to happen to her; but how this was she
could not have told. Nor could she have told why it was she
had sent Horace away. Perhaps his father might not wish to
see him, perhaps he might prefer to explain to her alone the
cause of his absence. She felt the need of first seeing her
husband alone, though she could not tell why. It was a very
long drive. Out of the bustling City streets she came to streets
more showy, less encumbered, though perhaps scarcely less
crowded, and then to some which showed the lateness of the
season by shut-up houses and diminished movement, and
then to line after line of those dingy streets, all exactly like
each other, which form the bulk of London. There are so
many of them, and they are so indistinguishable. She looked
out of the hansom and noted them all as she drove on – but
yet as if she noted them not, as if it were they that glided by
her, as in a dream. Then she reached the suburbs, the roads

with the flowery names, houses buried in gardens, with trees appearing behind the high enclosing walls. This perhaps was the strangest of all. She could not think what he could want here, so far out of the world, until she recalled to herself the idea of an illness and an operation which had already faded out of her mind – for that, like every other explanation, was so strange, so much unlike all his habits. Her heart began to beat as the cab turned into the street, going slowly along to look for the special house, and she found herself on the point of arriving at her destination. Though she was so anxious to find her husband, she would now, if she could, have deferred the arrival, have called out to the driver that it was not here, and bidden him go on and on. But there could not be any mistake about it – there was the name of the house painted on the gate. It was a little gate in a wall, affording a glimpse of a pretty little garden shaded with trees inside. She would not let the cabman ring the bell, but got out first and paid him, and then, when she could not find any further excuse, rang it – so faintly at first that no sound followed. She waited, though she knew she could not have been heard, to leave time for an answer. Looking in under the little arch of roses to the smooth bit of lawn, the flowers in the borders, she said to herself that there was not very much taste displayed in the flowers – red geraniums and mignonette, the things that everybody had, and great yellow nasturtiums clustering behind – not very much taste or individuality, but yet a great deal of brightness, and the look as of a home; not lodgings, but a place where people lived. There were some garden-chairs about, and on a rustic table something that looked like a woman's work. How natural it all seemed, how peaceable! It was curious that he should be living in such a place. Perhaps, she said to herself, it was the house of some clerk of the better sort – someone who had known him in his early years, and had wished to be kind: and in good air, and out of the noise of the streets. She made all these explanations as she stood at the door waiting for some one to answer a ring which she knew very well could not have been heard – unable to understand her own strange pause, and the manner in which she dallied with her anxiety. But this could not last for ever. After she had waited more than the needful time she rang again, and presently the door was opened by an unseen spring, and she went in within the pretty enclosure. How pretty it was – only red geraniums and nasturtiums, it was true, but the soft odour of the mignonette, and the sunshine, and the silence – all so peaceful and so calm. There came over her a certain awe as she stepped across the threshold and closed behind her the garden-door. The windows were all open, the house-door open. Under the trees on the little lawn were two basket-chairs, and a white heap of muslin, which some woman must have been working at, on the table. Mrs Lycett-Landon felt like an intruder in this peaceful place. She said to herself at last that there must be some mistake, that it could not be here.

A housemaid, wiping her arms on her apron, came to the house-door – a round-faced, ruddy, wholesome young woman, just the sort of servant for such a place. No doubt there were two, cook and housemaid, the visitor said to herself, just enough for needful service. The young woman was smiling and pleasant, no forbidding guardian. She did not advance to meet the stranger, but stood waiting, holding her own place in the doorway. Her honest, open face confirmed the expression of peace and comfort that was about the house. The intruder came up softly, not able to divest herself of that sense of awe.

'Does Mr Lycett-Landon live here?' she said, almost under her breath.

'Yes, ma'am, but he's rather poorly this morning,' the housemaid said.

'He is at home then? Will you take me to him, please –'

'Oh, I don't think I can do that, ma'am. He's rather poorly; he's keeping his room. The doctor don't think that it's anything serious, but as master is not quite a young gentleman he says it's best to be on the safe side.'

'Is Mr Lycett-Landon your master?'

'Yes, ma'am,' with a little curtsey.

'Has he been ill long?'

'Oh, bless you, not at all. He has his 'ealth as well as could be wished; only a little bilious or that now and then, as gentlemen will be. They ain't so careful in what they eat and drink as ladies – that's what I always say.'

'He is only bilious then – not ill? not long ill? there has been no – operation?'

'Oh, bless you, nothing of the sort!' the young woman said, with the most evident astonishment.

Mrs Lycett-Landon put all these questions in a kind of dream. Something kept her from saying who she was. She felt a curious anxiety to find out all the details before she announced herself.

'I think he will see me,' she said, a little faintly. 'I have come a long way to see him. Take me to him, please.'

'Is it business, ma'am?' said the girl.

'Business? yes; you may say it is business. I am his – Take me to him at once, please.'

'Oh dear, I can't do that. I ask your pardon, but the last thing the doctor said was that he mustn't be troubled with no business.'

'But I must see him,' Mrs Lycett-Landon said.

'You can't, ma'am, not today – it's not possible. To be sure,' the girl added with a pleasant smile, 'if Mrs Landon would do as well.'

'Mrs –, whom –?'

'Mrs Landon – Mrs Lycett-Landon, that's her full name. Oh, didn't you know as he was married? She'll be down in a moment if you'll step inside.'

The woman outside the door felt herself turned to stone. She said faintly, 'Yes, I think I will step inside.'

'Do, ma'am: you don't look at all well; you've been standing in the sun. Missis will be fine and angry if she knows as I let you stand like that. Take a chair, ma'am, please. She'll be here in a moment,' the cheerful maid-servant said.

She did not ask for the visitor's name – she was evidently not accustomed to visits of ceremony – but went upstairs quickly, with her solid foot sounding on every step.

The visitor for her part sat down, not feeling able to keep upon her feet, and faintly looked round her, seeing every-thing, understanding nothing. What did it all mean? The room was furnished like that of a newly-married pair. Little decorations were about, newly-bound books, a new little desk all ormolu and velvet; albums, photograph-frames, trifles from Switzerland, carved and painted, like relics of a recent journey. Nothing was in absolute bad taste, but the fashion of the furnishing was not of the larger kind, which means wealth. It was slightly pretty, perhaps a little tawdry, yet not sufficiently worn to acquire that look as yet. Mingled with all this decoration, however, there was something else which had a curious effect upon the intruder, something that reminded her of her husband's library at home, a chair of the form he liked, a solid table or two, strangely out of place amid the little low sofas and *etagères*. She saw all this, and took it into her mind at a glance, without making any of these observations upon it. She made no observations. She was unable even to think; the maid's words went through her head without any will of hers – 'Didn't you know as he was married?' 'If Mrs Landon would do as well.' Mrs Landon! Who was this that bore her own name – who was the man upstairs? She was not in any hurry to be enlightened. She seemed to herself rather grateful for the pause; glad to hold off any discovery that there might be to make with both hands, to keep it at arm's length. She sat quite still in this strange room, not thinking or able to think, wondering what was about to happen – what strange thing was coming to her.

At last she heard a footstep, a light step very different from the maid's, coming downstairs. She rose up instinctively and took hold of the back of a chair to support herself. The door opened, and a young woman, pretty, timid, tall, in a white flowing gown, with a little cap upon her dark hair, and a pair of appealing eyes, came in. She had an uncertain look, as if not wholly accustomed to her position. She said with a pretty blush and shyness, 'They tell me that you want to see my husband on business – but he is not well enough for business. Is it anything that I could do?'

'Will you tell me who you are?'

The newcomer looked a little surprised at the voice, which was hoarse and unnatural, of her visitor. She answered with a little dignity, drawing up her slight young figure. 'I am Mrs Lycett-Landon,' she said.

CHAPTER SIX

PERPLEXITIES

What was she to do?

It is not often in life that a woman is brought to such an emergency without warning, without time for preparation. She did nothing at all at first, and felt capable of nothing but to stare blankly, almost stupidly, at her supplanter. She did not feel capable even of rising from the chair into which she had sunk in the utter blank of consternation. She could only gaze, interrogating not the face before her only, but heaven and earth. Was it true? Could it be true?

The young woman was evidently surprised by this pause. She too looked curiously at her visitor, waited for a minute, and then advancing a step, asked, with a tone in which there was some surprise and a faint shadow of impatience, 'Is it anything that I can do?'

'Have you been married long?' This was all the visitor could say.

A pretty blush came over the other's face. 'We were married in the end of April,' she said. It still seemed quite natural to her that everybody should be interested in this great event.

'We went abroad for a month. And we were so lucky as to find this house. You know my husband?'

'I think so – well; his Christian name is –'

'Robert is his Christian name. Oh, I am so glad to meet with any one who has known him!' She drew a chair with a pretty vivacious movement close to that on which her visitor sat. 'I feel sure,' she said, 'you are a relation, and have come to find out about us.'

There was something in the young creature's air so guileless, so assured in her innocence, that if there had been any fury in the other's heart, or on her tongue, it must have been arrested then; but there was no fury in her heart. After the first unspeakable shock of surprise there was nothing but a great pang, and that almost more for this young life blighted than for her own. 'It is true,' she said, 'that I am a – connection. Is your mother alive?'

'Mamma?' cried the girl, with a laugh. 'Oh yes, and she is here today. She does not live with us, you know. She would not. She says married people should be left to themselves, though I always told her Mr Landon was far too sensible to believe in that trash about mothers-in-law. Don't you think it is rubbish? Young men may believe it; but when a gentleman is experienced and knows the world –'

'Perhaps I could see your mother,' said the old wife. She felt herself growing a little faint. The day was warm, and she had been travelling all night. Was not that enough to account for it? And this happy babble in her ear made her heart sick, which was more.

'Mamma? Oh yes, certainly she will be very glad to see you.

She always wanted to see some of the relations. She said it was not natural; though, to be sure, at his age – Shall I go and tell her you want to see her – her and not me? But you must not take any prejudice against me. Don't, please, if you are his relation: and you look so nice too. I know I should love you if you would let me.'

'Let me see your mother. I have no – prejudice.' She scarcely knew what she was saying. The room was swimming in her eyes, the green of the closed blinds waving up and down, surrounding her with an uncertain mist of colour, through which she seemed to see a half-reproachful, wondering look. And then the white figure was gone. Mrs Lycett-Landon leant her head upon the back of the chair, and for a minute knew nothing more. Then the greenness became visible again, and gradually everything wavered and circled back into its place.

The little house was very still; there were hurried steps overhead, as if two people were moving about. It was the mother hastily being put in order for a visitor – her cap arranged, a clean collar put on, the young wife dancing about her in great excitement to make all nice. This process of decoration occupied some time, and as it went on the visitor came fully to herself. What should she do? As she recovered full command of herself she shrunk from inflicting such a blow even upon the mother. Should she go away before they came down? – disappear like a dream, take no notice, but leave the strange little drama – what was it, comedy or tragedy? – to work itself out? Why should she interfere, after all? If he liked this best – and all the harm was now done that could be done – the best thing was to go away and take no more notice. She had risen with this intention to slip away, to let herself out, not to interfere, when another sound became audible – the sound of a door opening in the back part of the house. Then a voice called 'Rose' – a voice which, in spite of herself, made the visitor's brain swim once more. She had to stop again perforce. And then a step came towards the room in which she was; a heavy step, with a little gouty limp in it – a step she knew so well. It came along the passage, accompanied by a running commentary of half-complaint. 'Where are you? I want you.' Then the door of the little drawing-room was pushed open. 'Why don't you answer me?' He paused there in the doorway, seeing a stranger – with a quick apology – 'I beg your pardon.' Then suddenly there came from him a cry – a roar like that of a wounded animal – 'ELEANOR!'

Neither of the two ever forgot the appearance of the other. She saw him with the little passage and its stronger light opening behind him, his large figure relieved against it; the sudden look of consternation, horror, utter amazement in his face. Horror came first; and then everything yielded to the culprit's sense of unspeakable downfall, guilt self-convicted and without excuse. He fell back against the wall; his jaw dropped; his eyes seemed to turn upon themselves in a flicker of mortal dismay. The entire failure of all force and self-defence did not disarm his wife, as might have been supposed, but filled her with a blaze of sudden vehemence, passion which she could not contain. She had said his name as he said hers, in a quiet tone enough; but now stamped her foot and cried out, feeling it intolerable, insupportable. 'Well!' she cried, 'stand up for it like a man! Say you are sick of me, of your children, of living honestly these fifty years. Say something for yourself. Don't stand there like a whipped child.'

But the man had nothing to say. He stood against the wall and looked at her as if he feared a personal assault. Then he said, 'She is not to blame. She is as innocent as you are.'

'I have seen her,' said the injured wife. 'Do you think you need to tell me that? But then, what are you?'

He made no reply. And the sight of him in the doorway was unbearable to the woman. If he had stood up for himself, made a fight of any kind, it would have been more tolerable. But the very sight of him was insupportable – something she could not endure. She turned her head away and went quickly past him towards the open door. 'I meant to tell her mother.' She scarcely knew whether she was speaking or only thinking. 'I meant to tell her mother, but I cannot. You must manage it your own way.'

Next moment she found herself out in the street, walking along under the shadow of the blank wall. She was conscious of having closed both doors behind her, that of the house and that of the garden. If she could but have closed the door of her own mind, and put it out of sight, and shut it up for ever! She hurried away, walking very quickly round one corner after another, through one street after another, of houses enclosed in walls and railings, withdrawn among flowers and trees. You may walk long through these quiet places without finding what she wanted – a cab to take her out of this strange, still, secluded town of villas. When she found one at last, she told the driver to take her back to the Euston, but first to drive round Hyde Park. He thought she must be mad. But that did not matter much so long as she was able to pay the fare. And then there followed what she had wanted, a long, endless progress through a confusion of streets, first quiet, full of gardens and retired houses; then the long bustling thoroughfares leading back into the noisy world of London; then the quiet streets on the north side of the park, the trees of Kensington Gardens, the old red palace, the endless line of railings and trees on the other side; the bustle of Piccadilly, so unlike the bustle of the other streets. Naturally the hansom could not go within the enclosure of the park, but only by the streets. But she did not care for that. She wanted movement, the air in her face, silence so that she might think.

So that she might think! But a woman can no more think when she wills than she can be happy when she wills. All that she thought was this, going over and over it, and back and back upon it, putting it involuntarily into words and saying them to herself like a sort of dismal refrain. At fifty! After living honestly all these fifty years! Was it possible? was it in the heart of man? At fifty, after all these years! This wonder was so great that she could think of nothing else. And he had been a good man – kind, ready to help; not hard upon any one – fond of his family, liking to have them about him. And now at fifty! after living honestly – She did not think of it as a matter affecting herself, and she could not think of what she was to do, which was the thing she had intended to think of, when she bade the man drive to the other end of the world. When she perceived, as she did dimly in the confusion of her mind, that she was approaching the end of her long round, she would but for very shame have gone over it all again. But by this time she had begun to see that little would be gained by staving it off for another hour, and that sooner or later she must descend from that abstract wandering, which had been more like a wild flight into space than anything else, and meet the realities of her position. Ah heavens! the realities of her position were – first of all, Horace, her boy – her grown-up boy: no longer a child to whom a family misfortune could be slurred over, but a man, able to understand, old enough to know. Her very heart died within her as this suddenly flashed upon her deadened intelligence. Horace and Milly – a young man and a young woman. How was she to tell them what their father had done? At fifty! after all these years!

She was told at the hotel that the young gentleman had gone out – for which she was deeply thankful – but would be back immediately. Oh, if he might but be detained; if something would but happen to keep him away! She came up the great vulgar common stairs which so many people trod, some perhaps with hearts as heavy as hers, few surely with such a problem to resolve. How to tell her boy that his father – oh God! his father, whom he loved and looked up to; his kind father, who never grudged him anything; a man so well known; a good man, of whom everybody spoke well – to tell him that his father – She locked the door of her room instinctively, as if that would keep Horace out, and keep her secret concealed.

It was one of those terrible hotel rooms, quite comfortable and wholly unsympathetic, in which many of the sorest hours of life are passed, where parents come to part with their children, to receive back their prodigals, to look for the missing, to receive tidings of the worse than dead; where many a reconciliation has to be accomplished, and arrangement made that breaks the heart. Strange and cold and miserable was the unaccustomed place, with no associations or soothing, no rest or softness in it. She walked about it up and down, and then stopped, though the movement gave her a certain relief, lest Horace should come to the door, hear her, and call out in his hearty young voice to be admitted. She had not been able to think before for the recurrence of that dismal chorus, 'At fifty!' and now she could not think for thinking that any moment Horace might come to the door. She was more afraid of her boy than of all the world beside: had someone come to tell her that an accident had happened, that he had broken an arm or a leg, it seemed to her that she would have been glad, – anything rather than let him know. And yet he would have to know. The eldest son, a man grown, after his father the head of his family, the one who would have to take care of the children. How would it be possible to keep this from him? And how could it be told? His mother, who had prided herself on her son's spotless youth, and rejoiced in the thought that a wanton word was as impossible from the lips of Horace as from those of Milly, reddened and felt her very heart burn with shame. How could she tell him? She could not tell him. It was impossible; it was beyond her power.

And then she shrank into the corner of her seat and held her breath: for who could this be but Horace, with a foot that scarcely seemed to touch the ground, rushing with an anxious heart to hear news of his father, up the echoing empty stair?

CHAPTER SEVEN

EXPLANATION

'Mother! are you there? Let me in. Mother! open the door.'

'In a moment, Horace; in a moment.' It could not be postponed any longer. She rose up slowly and looked at herself in the glass to see if it was written in her face. She had not taken off her bonnet or made any change in her outdoor dress, and she was very pale, almost ghastly, with all the lines deepened and drawn in her face, looking ten years older, she thought. She put her bonnet straight with a woman's instinct, and then slowly, reluctantly, opened the door. He came in eager and impatient, not knowing what to think.

'Did you want to keep me out, mother? Were you vexed not to find me waiting? And how about papa?'

'No, Horace, not at all vexed.'

'I went a little farther than I intended. I don't know my way about. But, mother, what of papa?'

'Not very much, my dear,' she said, turning away. 'It must be nearly time for lunch.'

'Yes, it is quite time for lunch; and you had no breakfast. I told them to get it ready as I came up. But you don't answer me. Of course you found him. Is he really ill? What does he mean by it? Why didn't he come with you? Mother dear, is it anything serious? How pale you are! Oh, you needn't turn away; you can't hide anything from me. What is the matter, mamma?'

'It is serious, and yet it isn't serious, Horace. He is not ill, which is the most important thing. Only a little – seedy, as you call it. That's a word, you know, that always exasperates me.'

'Is that all?' the youth said, looking at her with incredulous eyes.

She had turned her back upon him, and was standing before the glass, with a pretence of taking off her bonnet. It was easier to speak without looking at him. 'No, my dear, that is not all. You will think it very strange what I am going to say. Papa and I have had a quarrel, Horace.'

'Mother!'

'You may well be startled, but it is true. Our first quarrel,' she said, turning half round with the ghost of a smile. It was the suggestion of the moment, at which she had caught to make up for the impossibility of thinking how she was to do it. 'They say, you know, that the longer one puts off a thing of this kind the more badly one has it, don't you know? – measles and other natural complaints. We have been a long time without quarrelling, and now we have done it badly.' She turned round with a faint smile; but Horace did not smile. He looked at her very gravely, with an astonishment beyond words.

'I cannot understand,' he said, almost severely, 'what you can mean.'

'Well, perhaps it is a little difficult; but still such things do happen. You must not jump at the conclusion that it is all my fault.'

Horace came up to her with his serious face, and put his arm round her, turning her towards him. 'I was not thinking of any fault, mother; but surely I may know more than this? You and he don't quarrel for nothing, and I am not a child. You must tell me. Mother, what is the matter?' he said, with great alarm. For she was overdone in every way, worn out both body and mind, and when she felt her son's arm round her nature gave way. She leant her head upon his young shoulder, and fell into that convulsive sobbing which it is so alarming to bear. It was some time before she could command herself enough to reply –

'Oh, that is true – that is true! not for nothing. But, dear Horry, you can't be the judge, can you, between your father and mother? Oh no! Leave it a little; only leave it. It will perhaps come right of itself.'

'Mother, of course I can't be the judge; but still, I'm not a child. May I go, then, and see papa?'

'Oh no,' she cried, involuntarily clasping his arm tight – 'oh no! not for the world.'

The youth grew very grave: he withdrew his arm from her almost unconsciously, and said, 'Either it is a great deal more serious than you say, or else –'

'It is very serious, Horace. I don't deceive you,' she said. 'It may come to *that* – that we shall never – be together any more. But still I implore you, don't go to your father – oh! not now, my dear. He would not wish it. You must give me your word not to go.'

She could not bear the scrutiny of his eyes. She turned and went away from him, putting off her light cloak, pulling open drawers as if in a search for something; but he stood where she had left him, full of perplexity and trouble. A quarrel between his parents was incredible to Horace; and the idea of a rupture, a public scandal, a thing that could be talked about! He stood still, overwhelmed by sudden trouble and distress, though without the slightest guess of the real tragedy. 'I can't think what you could quarrel about,' he said. 'It seems a mere impossibility. Whatever it is, you must make it up, mother, for our sakes.'

'My dear, anything that can be done, you may be sure will be done, for your sakes.'

'But it is impossible, you know. A quarrel! between you and papa! It is out of the question. Nobody would believe it. I think you must be joking all the time,' he said, with an abrupt laugh. But his laugh seemed so strange, even to himself, that he became silent suddenly with a look of confusion and irritation. Never in his life had he met with anything so extraordinary before.

'I am not joking,' she said; 'but, perhaps, after a while – Come and have your luncheon, Horace. I know you want it. And perhaps after a time –'

'You are worn out too, mother; that is what it is. One feels irritable when one is tired. After you have eaten something and rested yourself, let me go to papa. And we'll have a jolly dinner together and make it all up.'

And she had the heroism to say no more, but went down with him, and pretended to eat, and saw him make a hearty meal. While she sat thus smiling at her boy, she could not but wonder to herself what *he* was doing. Was he smiling too, keeping up a cheerful face for the sake of the unfortunate girl not much older than Horace? God help her whom he had destroyed! She kept imagining that other scene while she enacted her own. Afterwards she persuaded Horace with some difficulty to let everything stand over till next day, telling him that she had great need of rest (which was true enough) and would lie down; and that next evening would be time enough for any further steps. She insisted so upon her need of rest, that he remembered that Dick Fareham had asked him to dine with him at his club, and go to the theatre if he had nothing better to do – a plan which she caught at eagerly.

'But how can I go and leave you alone in a hotel?' he said.

'My dear, I am going to bed,' she replied, which was un-answerable. And after many attempts to know more, and many requests to be allowed to go to his father, Horace at last yielded, dressed, and went off to the early dinner which precedes a play. He had brought his dress clothes with him, though there had been so little time for feasting, confident that even a few days in London must bring pleasure of some kind. And already the utterly absurd suggestion that his father and mother could have had a deadly quarrel began to lose its power in his mind. It was impossible. His mother was worn out, and had been irritable; and his father, especially when he had a touch of gout, was, as Horace well knew, irritable also. Tomorrow all that would have blown away, and they would both be ashamed of themselves. Thus he consoled himself as he went out; and as the youth never had known what family strife or misfortune meant, and in his heart felt anything of the kind to be impossible, it did not take much to drive that incomprehensible spectre away.

Mrs Lycett-Landon was at length left alone to deal with it by herself. What was she to do? She had a fire lighted in the blank room, though it was the height of summer, for agitation and misery had made her cold, and sat over it trembling, and trying to collect her thoughts. Oh, if it could be but possible to do nothing, to say no word to anyone, to forget the episode of this morning altogether! 'If I had not known,' she said to herself, 'it would have done me no harm.' This modern Eleanor, who had fallen so innocently into Rosamond's bower, had no thought of vengeance in her heart. She had no wish to kill or injure the unhappy girl who had come between her and her husband. What good would that do? Were Rosamond made an end of in a moment, how would it change the fact? What could ever alter that? The ancients did not take this view of the subject. They took it for granted that when the intruder was removed life went on again in the same lines, and that nothing was irremediable. But to Mrs Lycett-Landon life could never go on again. It had all come to a humiliating close; confusion had taken the place of order, and all that had been, as well as all that was to be, had grown suddenly impossible. Had she not stopped herself with an effort, her troubled mind would have begun again that painful refrain which had filled her mind in the morning, which was perhaps better than the chaos which now reigned there. So far as he was concerned she could still wonder and question, but for herself everything was shattered. She could neither identify what was past nor face what was to come. Everything surged wildly about her, and she found no footing. What was to be done? These words intensify all the miseries of life – they make death more terrible, since it so often means the destruction of all settled life for the living, as well as the end of mortal troubles for the dead – they have to be asked at moments when the answer is impossible. This woman could find no reply as she sat miserable over her fire. She was not suffering the tortures of jealousy, nor driven frantic with the thought that all the tenderness which ever was hers was transferred to another. Perhaps her sober age delivered her from such reflections; they found no place at all in the tumult of her thoughts; the questions involved to her were wholly different: what she was to do; how she was to satisfy her children without shaming their youth and her own mature purity of matronhood which had protected them from any suggestion of such evil? How they were ever to be silenced and contented without overthrowing for ever in their minds their father and the respect they owed him? This was the treble problem which was before her – by degrees the all-absorbing one which banished every other from her thoughts. What could she say to Horace and Milly? How were they to be kept from this shame? Had they been both boys or both girls, it seemed to their mother that the question would have been less terrible; but boy and girl, young man and young woman, how were they ever to be told? How were they to be deceived and not told? Their mother's powers gave way and all her strength in face of this question. How was she to do it? How was she to refrain from doing it? That pretext of a quarrel, how was it to be kept up? and in what other way – in what other way, oh heaven! was she to explain to them that their father and she could meet under the same roof no more? She covered her face with her hands, and wept in the anguish of helplessness and incapacity; then dried her eyes, and tried again to plan what she could do. Oh that she had the wings of a dove, that she might flee away and be at rest! – but whither could she flee? She thought of pretending some sudden loss of money, some failure of fortune, and rushing away with the children to America, to Australia, to the end of the world; but if she did so, what then? Would it become less necessary, more easy to explain? Alas! no; nothing could change that horrible necessity. The best thing of all, she said to herself, if she were equal to it, would be to return home, to live there as long as it was possible, with her heart shut up, holding her peace, saying nothing – as long as it was possible! – until circumstances should force upon her the explanation which would have to be made. Let it be put off for weeks, for months, even for years, it would have to be made at last.

Thus she sat pondering, turning over everything, considering and rejecting a thousand plans; and then, after all, acted upon a sudden impulse, a sudden rising in her of intolerable loneliness and insufficiency. She felt as if her brain were giving way, her mind becoming blank, before this terrible emergency, which must be decided upon at once. Horace was safe for a few hours, separated from all danger, but how to meet his anxious face in the light of another day his mother did not know. She sprang up from her seat, and reached towards the table, on which there were pens and ink, and wrote a telegram quickly, eagerly, without pausing to think. The young ones were in the habit of laughing at old Fareham. She herself had joined in the laugh before now, and allowed that he was methodical and tedious and tiresome. He was all these, and yet he was an old friend, the oldest friend she had, one who had known her father, who had seen her married, who had guided her husband's first steps in the way of business. He was the only person to whom she could say anything. And he was a merciful old man: when troubles arose – when clerks went wrong or debtors failed – Mr Fareham's opinion was always on the side of mercy. This was one of the reasons why they called him an old fogey in the office; always – always he had been merciful. And it was this now which came into her mind. She wrote her telegram hastily, and sent it off at once, lest she should repent, directing it not to the office, where it might be opened by some other hand than his, but to his house. 'Come to me directly if you can. I have great need of your advice and help. Tell no one,' was what she said. She liked, like all women, to get the full good of the permitted space.

CHAPTER EIGHT

EXPEDIENTS

His mother was in bed and asleep when Horace returned from his play – or at least so he thought. He opened her door and found the room dark, and said, 'Are you asleep, mamma?' and got no answer, which he thought rather strange, as she was such a light sleeper. But, to be sure, last night had been so disturbed, she had not slept at all, and the day had been fatiguing and exciting. No doubt she was very tired. He retired on tiptoe, making, as was natural, far more noise than when he had come in without any precaution at all. But she made no sign; he did not wake her, where she lay, very still, with her eyes closed in the dark, holding her very breath that he might not suspect. Horace had enjoyed his evening. The play had been amusing, the dinner good. Dick Fareham, indeed, had asked a few questions.

'I suppose you found the governor all right?' he said.

'I didn't,' said Horace; 'the mother did.'

'And he's all right, I hope?'

'I can't tell you,' said Horace, shortly; 'I said I hadn't seen him.'

The conversation had ended thus for the moment, but young Fareham was too curious to leave it so. He asked Horace when he was coming to the London office. 'I know I'm only a warming-pan,' he said, 'keeping the place warm for you. I suppose that will be settled while you are here.'

'I don't know anything about it,' said Horace. 'We heard you were all at sixes and sevens in the office.'

'I at sixes and sevens!'

'Oh, I don't mean to be disagreeable. We heard so,' said Horace, 'and that the governor had his hands full.'

'I'd like to know who told you that,' said the young man. 'I'd like to punch his head, whoever said it. In the first place, it is not true, and your father is not the man to put such a story about.'

Now Horace had not been told this as the reason of his father's absence, but had found it out, as members of a family find out what has been talked of in the house, the persons in the secret falling off their guard as time goes on. He was angry at the resentment with which he was met, but a little at a loss for a reply.

'Perhaps you think I have put it about?' he said, indignant. 'It has not been put about at all, but we heard it somehow. That was why my father –'

'I think I can see how it was – I think I can understand,' said young Fareham. 'That was what called your father up to London. By Jove!'

And after that he was not so pleasant a companion for the rest of the evening. But the play was amusing, and Horace partially forgot this *contretemps*. When he found his mother's room shut up and quiet, he went to his own without any burden on his mind. He was not so anxious about 'the governor' as perhaps Milly in his place might have been. It was highly unpleasant that the mother and he should have quarrelled, and quite incomprehensible. But Horace went to bed philosophically, and the trouble in his mind was not enough to keep him from sleep.

Young Fareham, on his side, wrote an indignant letter to his uncle, demanding to know if his mind too had been poisoned by false reports. The young man was very angry. He was being made the scapegoat; he was the excuse for old Landon's absence, who had not been near the office for months, and he called upon his own particular patron to vindicate him. Had his private morals been attacked he might have borne it; but to talk of the office as at sixes and sevens! this was more than he could bear.

Next morning, before anybody else was awake, an early housemaid stole into Mrs Lycett-Landon's room, and told her that a gentleman had arrived who wanted to see her. The poor lady had slept a little towards the morning, and was waked by this message. She thought it must be her husband, and after a moment of dolorous hesitation got up hastily and dressed herself, and went to the sitting-room, which was still in the disorder of last night, and looking, if that were possible, still more wretched, raw, and unhome-like than in its usual trim. She found, with a great shock and sense of discouragement, old Mr Fareham, pale after his night's journey, with all the wrinkles about his eyes more pronounced, and the slight tremor in his head more visible than ever. He came forward to meet her, holding out both his hands.

'What can I do for you?' he said. 'What has happened? I came off, you see, by the first train.'

'Oh, Mr Fareham, I never expected this! You must have thought me mad. I think, indeed, I must have been off my head a little last night. I telegraphed, did I? – I scarcely knew what I was doing –'

'You have not found him, then?'

She covered her face with her hands. To meet the old man's eyes in the light of day and tell her story was impossible. Why had not she gone away, buried herself somewhere, and never said a word?

'I have seen Mr Landon, Mr Fareham; he is not – ill: but Horace knows nothing,' she said, hastily.

'My dear lady, if I am to do anything for you I must know.'

'I don't think there is anything to be done. We have had a – serious disagreement; but Horace knows nothing,' she repeated again. He looked at her, and she could not bear his eyes. 'I am very sorry to have given you so much trouble –'

'The trouble is nothing,' he said. 'I have known you almost all your life. It would be strange if I could not take a little trouble. I think I know what you mean. You were distracted last night, and sent for me. But now in the calm of the morning things do not look so bad, and you think you have been too hasty. I can understand that, if that is what you mean.'

She could not bear his eye. She sank down in the chair where she had sat last night and talked to Horace. *In the calm of the morning!* It was only now, when she felt that she had begun to live again, that all her problems came back to her, full awake, and fell upon her like harpies. *Things do not look so bad!* There passed through her mind a despairing question, whether she had strength to persuade him that this was so, and that there really was nothing to appeal to him about.

'My dear lady,' he said again, 'you must be frank with me. Is it a false alarm, and nothing for me to do? If so, not another word; I will forget that you ever sent for me. But if there is something more –'

How much was going through her mind, and how many scenes were rising before her eyes as he spoke! There appeared to her a vision of duty terrible to perform; of going home, putting on a face of calm, speaking of papa as usual to the children, living her life as usual, keeping her secret: and then of the universal questions that would arise, Where was he? what had become of him? why did he never return? Or she seemed to see herself going away, making some pretext of health, of education, she could not tell what, carrying her children, astonished, half unwilling, full of questions which she could not answer, away with her into the unknown. These visions rolled upward before her eyes surrounded with mists and confusion, out of which they appeared and reappeared. When her old friend stopped speaking her imagination stopped too, and she came to a pause. And then the impossibility of all these efforts came over her and overwhelmed her – the mists, the clouds, the chaos of helplessness and confusion in which there was no standing-ground, nor anything to grasp at, swallowing her up. She did not know how long she sat silent while the old man stood and looked at her. Then she burst forth all at once, –

'I cannot tell the children! How is it possible? Horace and Milly, they are grown up; they will want to know. How can I tell them? I want you to help me to keep it from them – to think of something. I would rather die than tell them,' she said, starting up wringing her hands.

'My dear lady! my dear lady! –'

'Mr Fareham, Robert – has married – again!'

The old man gave a loud cry – almost a shriek – of surprise and horror. 'You don't know what you are saying,' he said.

'That sounds as if I were dead,' she said, calmed by the revelation, with a faint smile. 'Oh yes, I know very well what I am saying. He is married – as if I were dead – as if I had never existed. I went to see him, and I saw – her!'

Old Fareham caught her hands in his; he led her to her seat again, and put her in it, uttering all the time sounds that were half soothing, half blaspheming. He stood by her, patting her on the shoulder, his old eyebrows contracted, his lips quivering under their heavy grey moustache. He was more agitated now than she was. The telling of her secret seemed to have delivered her soul. When he had recovered himself he asked a hundred questions, to all which she answered calmly enough. The room, with its look of disorder – the litter of last night, the fresh morning sunshine streaming in disregarded, emphasising the squalor of the ashes in the grate – surrounded with a fitting background the strange discussion between these two – the old man fatigued with his night journey, the woman pale as a ghost, with eyes incapable of sleep. She told him everything, forestalling his half-said protest that it must be another Lycett-Landon with the fact of her personal encounter with her husband, forgetting nothing. The facts of the case had by this time paled of their first importance to her eyes, while they were everything to his. They no longer agitated her; while that which convulsed her very soul seemed to him of but little importance. 'I cannot tell the children. How am I to tell the children?' He became weary of this refrain.

'We can think of the children later. In the meantime, this other is the important question. He has brought himself within the range of the law; you can punish him.'

'Punish him?' she said, with a strange smile – 'punish him?'

'Yes; you may forgive if you please, but I can't forgive. He deserves to be punished, and he shall be punished – and the woman –'

'He said she was as innocent – as I am.'

'He said! he is a famous authority. One knows what kind of creature –'

'I have seen her,' said Queen Eleanor, with a sigh, 'poor child. He said nothing but the truth; she is not in fault. She is the one who is most injured. I would save her if I could.'

'Save her! You would let this sweet establishment go on,' he said, with fine sarcasm, 'and not disturb them?'

'Yes,' she said. 'It may be wrong, but I think I would if I could.'

'You are mad!' cried the old man. 'You have lost all your good sense, and your feeling too. What, your own husband! you would let him go on living in sin – happy –'

She stopped him with a curious kind of authority – a look before which he paused in spite of himself.

'Happy!' she said; 'I suppose so; at fifty, after living honestly all these years!'

He stopped and shook his grey head. 'I have known such a thing before. It seems as if they must break out – as if common life and duty became insupportable. I have known such a case once before.'

She cried out eagerly, 'Who was it?' then stopped with a half-smile. 'What does it matter to me who it was? The only thing that matters now is the children. What is to be done about the children? I cannot tell them; nor can you, nor any one. Mr Fareham, let him alone; let him be – happy, as you call it – if he can. But the children – what am I to say to the children?' She rose up again, and began to walk about the room, unable to keep still. 'Horace, who is a man, and Milly. If they were little things it would not matter; they would not understand.'

'And is it possible,' said old Fareham, looking at her almost sourly, 'that this is the only thing you can think of? – not your own wrongs, nor his abominable behaviour, nor –'

She paused a little, standing by the table. 'Oh, you do wrong,' she said, 'you do wrong! A woman has her pride. If his duty has become – insupportable; it was you who used the word – and life insupportable, do you think a woman like me would hold him to it? Oh, you do wrong! I have put that away. But the children – I cannot put them away! And he was a good father, a kind father. Think of something. If only they might never find out!'

Here her voice gave way, and she could say no more.

'Horace will have to know,' he said, shaking his head.

'Why? You could tell him there was some difficulty between us, something that could not be got over. That we were both in the wrong, as people always are in a quarrel. And no doubt I must have been in the wrong, or – or Robert would never have gone so far – so far astray. No doubt I have been wrong; you must have seen it – you with your experience – and yet you never said a word. Why didn't you tell me? – you might have done it so easily. Why didn't you say, "You make life too humdrum, too commonplace for him. He wants variety and change?" I would have taken it very well from you. I am not a woman who will not take advice. Why did you never tell me? I could have made so many changes if I had known.'

He took her hand again, with a great pity, and almost remorse, in his old face. 'It is too early,' he said, 'to do anything. Tell me where I shall find him, and go back to your room and try to rest. Say you are too tired to see the boy, if that is all you are thinking of; and go to bed – go to bed, and try and get a little sleep. I have a great deal of experience, as you say. Leave it to me. I will see him, and then we will talk it over, and think what is best to be done.'

'You will see – him? What will you say to him, Mr Fareham? Why should you see him? Is not the chapter closed so far as he is concerned?'

'Closed? He will come home when he is tired of – the other establishment – is that what you mean him to do?'

She blushed like a girl, growing crimson to her hair. 'Oh yes,' she said, 'I know you have a great deal of experience; but, perhaps, here you do not understand. That – that would not be necessary. He is not a man who would – Mr Fareham, you don't suppose I wish him any harm?'

'You are a great deal too good – too merciful.'

'I am not merciful; it is all ended. Don't you know, since yesterday the world has come to an end. Life has become impossible – impossible! that is all about it. I am not angry; it is too serious for that. I would not harm him for the world. God help him! I don't know how he can live, any more than I know how I can live. It is – no word will express what it is. But he will not come back. He is not that kind of man!'

'Do you think if you had not seen him yesterday, if he did not know that you had found him out – do you think,' said old Fareham, deliberately, 'that he would not have come back?'

She looked at him for an instant, and then hid her face in her hands.

'I have no doubt on the subject,' said the old man, triumphantly. 'But when a man has put himself within the reach of the law he is powerless, and we have him in our hands.'

CHAPTER NINE

THE REVELATION

She woke suddenly with the sense that somebody was by her, and found Horace seated by her bed. She had fallen asleep in the brightness of the morning, overcome with fatigue, and also partly calmed by having confided her secret to another: even when it is painful, when it is indiscreet, it is always a relief. The bosom is no longer bursting with that which it is beyond its power to contain. She woke suddenly with that sense of some one looking at her which breaks the deepest sleep. She was still in her dressing-gown, lying upon her bed. 'Horace!' she said, springing up.

'I am so glad you have had a sleep. Don't jump up like that; you look so tired, mother, so worn out.'

'Not now, my dear; I feel quite fresh now. Did you enjoy your evening?'

'What does it matter about my evening?' he said, almost sternly. 'Mother, do you know that old Fareham came up by the night train?'

'Yes, Horace,' she said, turning her head away.

'You knew? Do you think you are treating me fairly – I that

am more interested than any one? What is the matter? The business has gone wrong. Do you mean to say that my father – *my* father –'

Poor Horace's voice faltered. That it should be *his* father was the extraordinary thing, as it always is full of mystery to us how misfortune, much less shame, should affect us individually. He looked at his mother with a look which was imperative and almost commanding, not perplexed and imploring, as it had been before. Mr Fareham's arrival had thrown light, as Horace thought, on the mystery – light which to him, as a young man destined to be a merchant prince, and to convey to the world higher ideas of commerce altogether, was more dreadful than anything else could have been. He thought he saw it all; and that as no one would be so deeply affected as he, his mother had been weakly trying to hide it from him. Horace felt that his spirit would rise with disaster, and that he was capable of raising the house again and all its concerns from the ground.

And for a moment she caught at this new idea. To her own feminine mind disaster to the business was as nothing in comparison with what had happened. If others could make him believe this, it would be a way out of the worse revelation. This was how she contemplated the matter. She said, 'It was I who sent for Mr Fareham. He is a very old friend, and his interests are all bound up with ours.'

'Then that is what it is. He has been speculating. Oh, how could you conceal such a thing from me? How could you keep me in the dark? Mother, I don't mean to be unkind, but this is nothing to you in comparison with what it is to me. You don't care for a man's credit,' said Horace, rising and striding about the room, 'or the reputation of the firm, or anything of real importance, in comparison with his health or his comfort or some personal matter. His health – of what consequence is that in comparison? Mother, mother, I shall find it hard to forgive you if you have let our credit be put in danger without warning *me*.'

This reproach was one that she had not looked for, and that took her entirely by surprise. She looked up at him, still feeling that what there was to say was worse, far worse than anything he could imagine, yet startled and confused by his vehemence. 'I – I – don't think the credit of the house will suffer,' she said, faltering a little.

'It is not so bad as that? But then why did you send for old Fareham? You ought to have taken no step without consult-ing me. I understand this sort of thing better than you do,' he said, with an impatience which he could not suppress. 'Mamma, I beg your pardon; everything else I am sure you know better – but the business! Don't you know I have been brought up to that? I mind nothing so much as the credit of the house.'

'Nothing, Horace?' she said, faintly.

'Nothing,' he repeated with vehemence, 'nothing! Of course,' he added after a moment, 'if papa were ill I should be very sorry: but he must not play with our credit, mother – he must not; that is the one thing. What has he been doing? Surely not anything to do with those new bubble companies?'

'Oh, Horace, how can I tell you? Wait till Mr Fareham comes back.'

'He has gone to see papa, then? I thought it must be that; but why, why not tell me? I am not very old, perhaps, but I know about the business, and care more for it than any one else. I would make any sacrifice, but our credit must not be touched – it must not be touched.'

'Compose yourself, Horace; it need not be touched, so far as I can see.'

This calmed him a little, and he sat down by her, and took pains to explain his views to her. 'You see, mamma,' he said kindly, but with a little natural condescension, 'ladies have such a different way of looking at things. You think of health and comfort and good temper, and all that, when a man thinks of his affairs and his reputation. You would be more distracted if the governor' (at home Horace never ventured on this phrase, but it suited the atmosphere of town) 'had a bad accident, or got into a snappish state, than if he had pledged the credit of the firm. It is nice in you to think so, but it would be silly in a man.'

'You think then, Horace, that nothing can be so bad as trouble to the firm. You think that loss of –?'

'Loss of money is not everything,' he said, testily. 'I hope Lycett-Landon's could lose a lot of money without being much the worse. The fact is, you don't understand. It is always the personal you dwell upon. I am not reproaching you, mamma; it is your nature.' He patted her hand as he said this, and looked at her with a half smile of boyish wisdom and superiority, very kindly compassionating her limited powers.

This silenced her once more: and so they remained for some time, he sitting thoughtfully by her, she reclining on the bed looking at him, trying to read the meaning in his face. At last she said tremulously, 'I am not quite so bad as you think: but perhaps a matter that touched our family peace, that sundered us from each other – disunited us –'

He kept on patting her hand, but more impatiently than before. 'Nothing could do that – permanently,' he said. And he asked no more questions. He was a little, a very little, contemptuous of his mother. 'I ought to have gone along with old Fareham. We should have talked it over together. I suppose now I must have patience till he comes back. When do you think he will come back? Can't I go and join him there? Oh, you think papa wouldn't like it? Well, perhaps he might not. It is rather hard upon me, all the same, to wait on and know nothing.'

'Don't you think if you were to take a walk, Horace, or go and see the pictures –?'

'Oh, the pictures! in this state of anxiety? Well, yes, I think I will take a walk; it is better than staying indoors. And don't you make yourself unhappy, mother. It can't have been going on very long, and no doubt we shall pull through.'

Saying this with a cloudy smile, Horace went away, waving his hand to her as he went out. She then got up and dressed with a stupefied sensation, taking all the usual pains about her toilet, though with a sense that it was absolutely unimportant. She could not remember what day it was, or what month, or even what year. She was conscious of having received a remorseless and crushing blow, but that was all; when she had left home or whether she would ever go back to it, she could not tell; neither could she form the least idea of what was going to happen when old Mr Fareham came back. She forgot that she had not breakfasted, and even, what was more wonderful, that to save appearances it was necessary to make believe to breakfast. Everything of the kind was swept away. She went into the sitting-room and sat down at the window like an abstract woman in a picture. It was very strange to her to do nothing; and yet she never thought of doing anything, but sat down and waited – waited for something that was about to happen, not knowing what it might be.

She had not waited long when one of the hotel servants knocked at the door, and, opening it, admitted a stranger whom she had never seen before – a small, thin woman in a widow's dress, who stood hesitating, looking at her with a pair of anxious eyes, and for the first moment said nothing. Mrs Lycett-Landon was roused by the unlooked-for appearance of this visitor. She rose up, wondering, at such a moment, who it was that could have come to disturb her. The stranger was very timid and shy. She hung about the door as if there were a protection in being near it.

'I beg your pardon,' she said, 'I don't even know by what name to speak to you. But one of my daughter's maids saw you yesterday get into a cab, and then we heard you had come here.'

'I think I understand; your daughter is –?'

'Mrs Landon, madam, where you called yesterday. You asked for me, and then went away without seeing me. I could not help feeling anxious. You may think it presuming in me to track you out like this, but I do feel anxious. We were afraid perhaps that my son-in-law –'

She had a wistful, deprecating look, like that of a woman who had not received much consideration in the course of her life. She watched the face of the person she addressed with an anxiety which evidently was habitual, as if to see how far she might go, to avoid all possible offence. Mrs Lycett-Landon returned the look with one which was full of alarm, almost terror. It seemed impossible that she could get through this interview without revealing everything; and the small, anxious, hesitating figure looked so little able to bear any shock.

'Will you sit down?' she said, offering her a chair.

The stranger accepted it gratefully, with a timid smile of thanks. She seemed to take this little civility as a good omen, and brightened perceptibly. She was very carefully, neatly dressed, but her crape was somewhat rusty, and the black gown evidently taken much care of. She twisted her hands together nervously.

'We were afraid,' she repeated, 'that perhaps Mr Landon – had got himself into trouble with his own family because of his marriage; and that you had come perhaps – to see. We were so delighted that you should have come; and then when we found you had gone away –'

Her voice trembled a little as she spoke. She watched every movement of the face which regarded her with such strange emotion, ready to stop, to modify any word that displeased.

'Then did you let him – did you give him your daughter – without any inquiries, without knowing anything –?'

'Oh, madam,' the widow cried, clasping and unclasping her nervous hands, 'perhaps I was imprudent. But at his age one does not think of the family approving. If he had been a younger man – But who could have any right to interfere at his age?'

'That is true – that is very true!'

'And you see it came upon me, you might say, un-expectedly. I saw that he was getting fond of Rose; but I never thought, if you will excuse me for saying so, that she would marry a gentleman so much older – and then it was so sudden at the last. He had leave from his office, and the opportunity of getting away –'

'Leave from his office!' The listener could not help repeating this with a curious cry of indignation. It gave her a shock, in the midst of so many shocks. As for the widow, this interruption confused her. She trembled and stumbled in her simple tale.

'And so – and so – it was settled at last in a hurry. I have not very strong health, and I was very glad that Rose should be settled. Oh yes, I was glad that she should have some one to take care of her in case anything happened. I had confidence that you could feel for me as a mother; perhaps you are a mother yourself.'

The widow stopped short when she had made this sug-gestion, with a momentary panic; for Rose's idea had been that the lady who had appeared and disappeared so suddenly was a sister, perhaps a maiden sister. Her mother judged otherwise, but then paused, afraid.

'Yes, I am a mother myself.'

'I thought so – I thought so! and I felt sure you would feel for me as a mother. It was Rose I had to think of. As for his family, at his age, you will understand – But it makes my poor girl very unhappy to think she may have been the means of separating him from his relations. I tell her a wife is more to a man than any other relation. But still, if it could be possible to make a reconciliation – if you would be so kind as to help us –'

The nervous hands clasped together; the little hesitating woman looked with a face full of prayer and entreaty at the lady who sat there before her, like an arbiter of fate. If she could have known how the heart was beating in that lady's breast! Mrs Lycett-Landon did not speak for some time, not being able to command her voice. Then she said, tremulously, but with a great effort to be calm –

'You don't know what you ask. I am the last person –'

'Oh, madam!'

She had an old-fashioned, over-respectful way of using this word. And there was no fear or suspicion of the truth, though much anxiety, in her eyes.

'Oh, madam! you have a kind face; and who should be the one to make peace but such as you, that can feel for a young creature, and knows what is in a mother's heart?'

The words were scarcely out of her lips when Horace entered hastily, asking, before he saw that any stranger was present –

'Mother, has Fareham come back?'

'No, Horace; but you see I am engaged.'

'I beg your pardon,' he said, surprised by the look of agitation in the stranger's face. But he was terribly excited. 'I won't stay a moment; but do please tell me papa's address. I cannot wait and knock about all day. Old Fareham is so tedious; he will take hours about it. Tell me my father's address.'

Horace was not without wiles of his own. He thought it more likely that he should extract this address when somebody was there.

'Horace, I am engaged, as you can see.'

'Only a moment, mother; it was something flowery – Laburnum, or Acacia, or something. If I go to the office I can get it in a moment.'

The little widow rose up; something strange and terrible came over her face.

'Young gentleman,' she said, 'are you any relation to Mr Lycett-Landon? You will tell me if no one else will.'

'Relation!' said Horace, with a laugh, 'oh yes ; only his son, that is all!'

'And this lady ? This lady is –?'

'My mother; who else should she be?' the youth said.

There was a moment during which the two women stood gazing at each other in an awful suspension of all sound or thought. And then the visitor uttered a great and terrible cry, and fell down at their feet upon the floor.

CHAPTER TEN

THE END

The Lycett-Landons went home to The Elms that night.
Horace asked his mother no questions. He helped her to lift up
and place upon a sofa the visitor whose strength had failed
her so strangely; but how much he heard from Mr Fareham,
or how much he guessed, she never knew. He was anxious to
go home at once, and, instead of making any objections as
she had feared, facilitated everything. He was very kind and
tender to her on the journey, taking care of her and of her
comfort, saving her from every trouble. This had not hereto-
fore been Horace's way. He was still so young that the habit
of being taken care of was more natural to him than that of
taking care of others; but he had learned a new version
apparently of his duty on that strange and agitating day. It
was late when they reached the Mersey again, and the great
river was full of shooting fireflies, little steamers with their
sparks of glowing colour flitting and rustling to and fro
among the steady lights of the moored ships. The sky was pale
with the rising moon, the stars appearing languidly out of the
clouds. As they crossed the river to their home, sitting close

together on the deck, saying nothing to each other, avoiding in the darkness all contact with the other passengers, two or three little steam-boats rustled past, full of music and a crowd of merrymakers going home noisy and happy after a day's pleasure. The sky was stained all round the horizon behind them by the smoke of the great town, but before them was soft and clear with fringes of dark foliage and outlines of peaceful houses rising against it. Everything was full of quiet and peace, no false or discordant note anywhere; even the fiddles and flutes of the bands harmonised by the air and water and magical space about, and the dew dropping, and the moon rising. It was only forty-eight hours since they had left their home almost under the same conditions, but what a change there was!

Milly was full of questions and surmises. How was papa? Why did they leave him? When was he coming home? Why did they return so soon? She supposed the season was over, and nothing going on, not even the theatres. She never thought it possible they would come back directly. She poured a flood of remarks upon them as they walked from the boat to the house. Fortunately it was dark, and their faces gave her no information; but their brief replies, and a something indefinable, a restraint in the atmosphere about them, a something new which she did not understand, began to affect the girl after the first abandon of her surprise and her interrogations. As soon as Mrs Lycett-Landon entered the house she announced that she was very tired and going to bed. 'I am growing old; travelling affects me as it never used to do, and I have got a headache. I shall go to bed at once, Milly. No, I don't want anything to eat; quiet and rest – that is all I want. Give Horace his supper, dear; and you need not come into my room tonight. I shall put out my light and get to sleep.'

'Not even a cup of tea, mamma? Mayn't I come and help you to take off your things? Let me send White away, and undress you myself.'

'I want no one, my darling, neither you nor White. My head aches. I want darkness and quiet. Good night. Tomorrow morning I shall be all right.'

She kissed them, her veil still hanging over her face, and hurried upstairs. Milly watched her till she had disappeared, and then turned upon her brother. 'What does this mean?' said the girl; 'what has happened to mamma, and where's papa, Horry? Tell me this very moment, before you have your supper or anything. I know something must be wrong.'

'Something is wrong,' said Horace, 'but I can't tell you what it is. I don't know what it is. Now, Milly, that is all I am going to say. You need not go on asking and asking, for you will only make me miserable, I can't tell you anything more.'

'You can't tell me anything more?' She was struck, not dumb indeed with amazement, but into such a quiver and agitation that she could scarcely speak. Then she regained her courage a little. 'Where's papa? He can't be ill, or you would not have come home.'

'I have not seen him,' said Horace, doggedly.

'You have not seen him?'

'Mother did, and then old Fareham. I can tell you this: it isn't speculation, or anything of that sort. The firm is all right. It's nothing about that.'

'The firm – speculation!' cried Milly, with wild contempt. 'Who cares for business? What is the matter? and why doesn't he come home?'

'Who cares for it? I care for it. I thought at first that was what had happened; but we may make our minds quite easy – it's not that.' Horace was really comforted by this certainty, though not perhaps so much as he pretended to be. 'I was very much frightened at first,' he said. 'It was a great relief to find that, whatever it is, it is not that.'

Milly stood looking at him with scared eyes. 'Do you mean to say that papa is not coming home? Oh, Horry, for goodness' sake tell me something more. Has he done anything? What has he done? Papa! It is impossible, impossible!' the girl cried.

'So I should have said too,' said Horace, who had now had a long time in which to accustom himself to the idea. 'Perhaps the mother will tell you something; she has not said a word to me. I don't know, and therefore I can't tell you. It has been a horrid sort of day,' said the lad, 'and perhaps you'll think it unfeeling, Milly, but I'm hungry. I'd like to have something to eat, and then I'd like to go to bed. I'm horribly tired, too; wandering about, and always waiting to hear something and never hearing, and imagining all sorts of things, is very fatiguing, and I don't think I've eaten anything today.'

Milly despised her brother for thinking of eating, but yet it was a relief to superintend his supper and get him all he wanted. They had a great deal of talk over this strange meal, and though Horace gave his sister no information, they yet managed to assure themselves somehow that a terrible catastrophe had happened, and that their father had gone out of their lives. Milly wept bitterly over it, and even Horace could not keep the tears from his eyes; but somehow they recognised the fact between them, far more easily than their mother above stairs or any bystander could have imagined possible. Two days ago what could have been more impossible to them? And Milly did not know even so much as Horace knew, nor had any insight at all into how it was; and yet she, too, in the course of an hour or so, had accepted the fact. To youth there is something convincing in certainty, an obedience to what is, which is one of the most remarkable things in life. They acknowledged the mystery with wonder and pain, but they did not rebel or doubt. Their mother thought nothing less than that they would struggle, would be incredulous, would rebel even against her for their father's sake. But there was nothing of all this. They submitted almost without a struggle, though they did not understand.

And then the quiet days closed down upon this family, upon which so mysterious a loss had fallen. It need not be said that there was great discussion as to the cause of Mr Lycett-Landon's disappearance, both among the merchants in Liverpool and among their wives and daughters on the other side of the water. The explanations that were given at first were many and conflicting; and for a long time people continued to ask, 'When do you expect your husband?' or 'your father?' And then there came the time, not less painful, when people pointedly refrained from asking any questions, and changed the subject when his name was mentioned, which was, perhaps, almost less tolerable. Then, gradually, by degrees it became an old story, and people remembered it no more. Ah, yes! they remembered it whenever any incident happened in the family – when Horace took his place as one of the partners in the office, when Milly married – then it all cropped up again, with supposititious details; but when nothing was happening to them the family escaped into obscurity, and their circumstances were discussed no longer. Old Mr Fareham had a very bad cold after he returned from London, and was for some time confined to the house, and would see nobody. And then other things happened, as they are continually happening in a mercantile community. A great bankruptcy, with many exciting and disgraceful circumstances, followed soon after, and the attention of the community was distracted. The Lycett-Landon business remained a mystery, and after a while the waters closed tranquilly over the spot where this strange shipwreck had been.

Milly never heard till after her marriage what it was that had happened, and at no time did Horace ask any questions: how much he divined, how much he had been told, his mother never knew. And she herself never was aware how the other story ended: if the poor Rose, her husband's unfortunate young wife, died of it, or if she abandoned him; or if the poor mother lacked the courage to tell her; or if between them the young woman was kept in her poor little suburban paradise deceived. Mrs Lycett-Landon made many a furtive effort to ascertain how it had ended; but she was too proud to inquire openly, and though she wondered and pondered she never knew.

Years, however, after these events, when Horace had begun to be what he had determined upon being, a merchant prince, and the house of Lycett-Landon & Co (old Mr Fareham being dead, and young Mr Fareham at the head of the American branch, Landon, Fareham & Co) was greater than ever, Mr Lycett-Landon suddenly appeared at The Elms. He came to make a call in the morning, sending in his name; for the old butler was dead, and the new one did not know him, and he was admitted like any other stranger. His wife even did not know who he was – for she had come down expecting a distant relation – until she had looked a second or third time at the stout, embarrassed old gentleman, looking very awkward and deprecating, who stood up when she came into the room, and shrank with a certain confusion from her inspection. After the first shock of the recognition they sat down and conversed calmly enough. He inquired about the children with a little affectation of ease.

'I know about Horace, of course,' he said, 'and I saw Milly's marriage in the papers. But I should like to hear a little about the others.'

She accepted his curiosity as very natural, and gave him all the particulars very openly and sedately. He sat for nearly an hour, sometimes asking questions, sometimes listening, with a curious air of politeness, like a man on his best behaviour, in the society of a lady a little above him in station, and with whom his acquaintance was far from intimate, and then took his leave.

With what thoughts their minds were full as they sat there, in the old home equally familiar to both, where every article

of furniture, every picture on the walls, had the same associations to both! But nothing was said to betray the poignant
sensation with which the woman, compunctious, though
she had never been revengeful, or the man, so strangely
separated and fallen from all that had been habitual to
him, beheld each other, sat by each other, after these years.
He smiled, but she had not the strength to smile. After this,
however, he came again at intervals, always asking with
interest about his children, but not caring to see them.

'I suppose they don't remember anything about me,' he
said.

His visits were not frequent, but he became, in the end,
acquainted with all the family, and even resumed a certain
intercourse with Horace and Milly, his first meeting with
whom was accidental and very painful. To see him elderly,
stout, and (but perhaps this was one effect of some refinement
of jealous and wounded feeling on the part of Mrs Lycett-
Landon) oh so commonplace! and fallen from his natural
level, shuffling his feet, reddening, smiling that confused and
foolish smile, conciliating his children, gave to his wife almost
the keenest pangs she had yet suffered. She could not bear to
see him so lowered from his natural place. Tragedy is terrible,
but when it drops into tragi-comedy, tragi-farce at the end,
that is the most terrible of all. Pity, shame, something that
was like remorse, though she was blameless, was in his wife's
heart. The impulse in her mind was to go away out of the
house that was his, and leave him in possession. But, to do
him justice, he never, by look or word, reminded her that the
house had been his, or that he was anything but a visitor.

And what was the explanation of the strange passion which made him, at fifty, depart from all the traditions of his virtuous life – whether it was a passion at all, or only some wonderful, terrible gust of impatience, which made duty and the rule of circumstances, and all that he was pledged and bound to, insupportable – she never knew; nor whether he found that this poor game was even for a moment worth the blazing flambeau of revolution which it cost; or whether it cost him still more than that candle – the young life which he had blighted; whether Rose lived or died; or where he came from when he paid these visits to his old home, and disappeared into when they were over: all this Mrs Lycett-Landon lived in ignorance of, and so, in all probability, will die.

AFTERWORD

The two novellas in this volume are surprisingly un-Victorian. Each ends, not with a marriage as is usual, but with the break-up of a marriage. Each is about the terribly destructive effects of middle-aged passion.

Margaret Oliphant Wilson Oliphant (1828–97) was a once very famous writer, now much underrated. Most of the great nineteenth-century women novelists – Jane Austen, the Brontës, George Eliot – were childless. Mrs Gaskell had four daughters, but she also had a husband with a job. Mrs Oliphant was a single mother and the family breadwinner for most of her adult life.

All agree that she was an impressive woman. Contemporaries spoke of her dignified but extremely witty presence, her prematurely white hair and intense dark eyes, her habit of mixing freely by day and working for most of the night. 'She was of an intellect so alert,' wrote JM Barrie, 'that one wondered she ever fell asleep.' It was noticed, too, that she never complained about the many tragedies in her life. The novelist Howard Sturgis, who was at Eton with her sons, recalled, 'She had a friend . . . who was always big with sighs over her own departed happiness, and the cruelty with which the world had used her; and I remember even as a boy dimly apprehending the contrast between the two women, the greater nobility of Mrs Oliphant's attitude towards the past.'

Growing up in Liverpool with her Scottish parents, she discovered by the time she was twenty-one that she could make an income by writing, and from then on she hardly ever stopped. She married her cousin Frank Oliphant, a gifted artist, but they were probably not very happy, and three out of six babies died. When she was thirty-one Frank also died, of tuberculosis, leaving her to support her surviving children by grinding out novels and articles at a horrifying pace. Altogether she published one hundred and twenty-five full-length volumes (not to mention innumerable essays and book reviews). Not surprisingly, most of them are forgotten, but a few of her novels and short stories deserve to be remembered, including these.

Whenever her life seemed to be getting better, something went wrong. Her eldest child Maggie died at the age of ten; perhaps she was the inspiration for Mrs Blencarrow's delicate and much-loved daughter. And then her brother, Frank Wilson, a respectable family man of fifty-two, appeared to go mad. After working for many years at a bank in Birkenhead, he lost, or perhaps stole, some money, and decamped to France without his wife and children. 'It seems as if they must break out – as if common life and duty become insupportable,' as a character in *Queen Eleanor and Fair Rosamond* says wearily about middle-aged men. Margaret immediately paid his debts and took responsibility for him and his family. She would care for them, as well as her own two sons, for the rest of their joint lives.

The two stories were written in the late 1880s, when she had been a widow for many years and her brother had died. She was living in Windsor, round the corner from Queen Victoria, and looking after four young people in their twenties and thirties – two nieces and her sons, who behaved badly and never found jobs. She had no fixed income but was forced to write many millions of words in order to support them. Her responsibilities, like Mrs Blencarrow's, were very great.

You will not have had much trouble solving this particular mystery in *The Mystery of Mrs Blencarrow*. It is obvious that the mistress of the house has married one of her own servants, whose name happens to be Brown. What sophisticated readers would have known is that the story is based on the life of Queen Victoria, who, after Albert died, became devoted to her groom, John Brown (1826-83). He was a good-looking but rough sort of man, seven years younger than the Queen – but that was the least of her problems – whose roots were in the Scottish working class. She doted on him; he treated her quite unceremoniously. Their relationship (dramatised in the 1997 film *Mrs Brown*) was probably platonic, but that did not stop people claiming that they were secretly married or having an affair. Her children were furious and her courtiers appalled. If she had openly married him there would have been a monumental scandal and she might even have been certified insane.

Margaret Oliphant knew the gossip and had met the Queen occasionally. Years earlier she had felt impatient with her very public mourning for her husband: 'A woman is surely a poor creature if with a large happy affectionate family of children around her, she can't take heart to do her duty whether she likes it or not.' She herself, it has to be said, had recovered rather quickly from Frank Oliphant's death.

This is the background to the story of Mrs Blencarrow, a dignified woman of forty, with several children, whose life appears to be blameless and sexless. Although she has servants, she is not an idle woman but like Victoria administers a great estate. She is 'a princess in her way, a queen-mother', but she is also 'a woman with a fine constitution and in the prime of life'. Readers today may be perplexed by the shock and horror; why shouldn't she get married again to whomever she likes? As the clergyman, Mr Germaine, says, she has not actually done anything wrong. But the point is that in Mrs Blencarrow's world there would be an enormous scandal, and her brothers, who are joint guardians of the children, would take them away rather than let them be brought up by Brown.

That is the heart of the problem, because Mrs Blencarrow, like her creator, cares far more deeply for her children than for any man. She had once been in a similar position. There was never any scandal, but after her husband's death she made friends with Robert Story, an attractive man seven years younger than herself, who may have wanted to marry her. It seems that she decided against it, but was briefly tempted, and there are several hints in her fiction that she understood the feelings of a young widow who had not lost all interest in men.

So much has dated, yet the basic human problem remains the same. If a woman has children but no husband, does she put her own needs or her children's needs first? The Victorians tended to believe that if a widow remarried her children would suffer. Dickens had studied this problem in *David Copperfield*; Margaret Oliphant had studied it in *A Country Gentleman and his Family* (1886). In this novel, one of her finest, a woman who is devoted to her small son marries a younger man, and it turns out badly. Although there is no class difference, her new husband resents her child and the marriage breaks up.

She was not very good at constructing plots. It is barely credible that the silly young runaway bride, Kitty, just happens to find the name Blencarrow on the Gretna Green register – but does not notice Brown's name – and that the two brothers should look at the same record but fail to find it, 'by some chance, by some miracle – how could she tell what?' The mechanics did not interest her. The vital point is that Mrs Blencarrow, who is really Mrs Brown, saves her reputation but loses her husband – and both of them are intensely relieved when he clears off.

We understand why she found him attractive. He is handsome and vigorous, a brilliant skater, a useful 'half-steward, half-agent' who has been a great help to her. But the marriage has quite quickly gone bad, not only because she is older, in years and life-experience, but also because of the vast difference in status. It cannot be openly acknowledged and, of course, the man resents his position:

'I am not a gentleman,' he said, 'but I've married a lady. What have I made by it? At first I was a fool. I was pleased whatever she did. But that sort of thing don't last. I've never been anything but Brown the steward, while she was the lady and mistress. How is a man to stand that? I've been hidden out of sight. She's never acknowledged me, never given me my proper place. Brought up to supper at the ball by those two brats of boys, spoken to in a gracious sort of way, "My good Brown." And I her husband – her husband, whom it was her business to obey!'

Brown – who does not speak for himself until the penultimate chapter – is, as he says, no gentleman, but he has his standards. Legally he is entitled to everything she owns and everyone takes it for granted that her duty to her husband 'must come first'. He is sick of her and wants a wife of his own age and class, but does not expose her to her spiteful neighbours. Instead he goes away quietly and only one other person will ever know the secret of Mrs Blencarrow.

It will be seen (it is obvious in many other novels) that Margaret Oliphant did not have a romantic view of marriage. This novel ends with the young lovers, Kitty and Walter, settling into a relationship which, 'like most others', is not exactly happy or unhappy, while Mrs Blencarrow remains alone. The author has great sympathy with her, but her behaviour has been inappropriate and undignified. Her role is to be 'my children's guardian, their steward, their caretaker', and there will be no other man in her life. Having had her adventure she wants nothing but 'her children, and her home, and this perfect peace.'

The title of *Queen Eleanor and Fair Rosamond* comes from a famous legend of the twelfth century. Henry II certainly had a mistress called Rosamund Clifford, who perhaps had a love-nest at Woodstock, and it was said that Eleanor, his queen, tracked her down there and forced her to drink poison. This story is not true, but it does show how people expected a middle-aged wife to react to a younger, lovelier woman who had trespassed on her rights.

When she wrote the novella Margaret Oliphant was almost certainly thinking of her youth in Birkenhead and the extraordinary behaviour of her brother Frank in 1868. Eleanor, the central figure, can hardly believe that a man of that age can simply walk out on his responsibilities. We are invited to wonder at 'the strange passion which made him, at fifty, depart from all the traditions of his virtuous life.'

Mr and Mrs Lycett-Landon have been married for a quarter of a century and have a family of six. (Some of their other children have died, and she feels it more deeply than he does.) But the passion has gone out of their marriage, and the children have no real need of him:

It was rather a relief to them all when the father went away again. They did not say so indeed in so many words, still keeping up the amiable domestic fiction that the house was not at all like itself when papa was away. But as a matter of fact there could be little doubt

that the atmosphere was clear after he was gone . . .
There was nothing impassioned in their affection for
their father, and Mrs Lycett-Landon was happy with
her children, and quite satisfied that her husband
should do what he thought best.

She is so content without him, in fact, that it takes her
some time to realise that he is suffering from some sort of
monomania. His strange behaviour can mean nothing, surely,
'except business, or the good of the children, or some other
perfectly legitimate desire?' But it turns out that he has
illegitimate desires, and this eventually brings her to the
London suburbs, through the flowery streets, into the heart of
Rosamond's bower. Her husband has committed bigamy.

This may sound far-fetched. But some men did commit
bigamy, into the next century and beyond, and Margaret
stresses that the new young 'wife' is an innocent victim. She
would not have sympathised with a woman who had knowingly set up home with a married man. Rose has fallen in
love, as young people do, with the selfish and querulous Mr
Lycett-Landon, and after the first dreadful shock his wife is
prepared to let the situation go on:

> This modern Eleanor, who had fallen so innocently into
> Rosamond's bower, had no thought of vengeance in her
> heart. She had no wish to kill or injure the unhappy girl
> who had come between her and her husband. What
> good would that do? Were Rosamond made an end of
> in a moment, how would it change the fact?

The young woman will be heartbroken if she ever finds out; her reputation will be destroyed. For herself, Eleanor realises that her marriage is an empty shell and that she does not want the man back. As other women have done, she blames herself – 'No doubt I have been wrong' – and worries about protecting his reputation. But eventually she settles back into a quiet life with her children and, when she meets her husband again, has no feeling for him. He has messed up the lives of three women (for we must not forget Rose's mother), but he is no romantic hero, just an 'elderly, stout . . . oh so commonplace' man.

It is high time for this story, 'as terrible and grim a picture of a man tired of fifty years of respectability as was ever written', to come back into print. The words are those of J M Barrie, who went on, 'Mrs Oliphant wrote so many short stories that she forgot their names and what they were about, but readers, I think, will not soon forget this one.'

These two novellas were written within three or four years of each other and belong naturally together, as indeed Penelope Fitzgerald pointed out in 1995 when she observed about Mrs Oliphant that 'she is at her very best in novellas and short stories' and said that these two 'might well be reprinted together' (which is what Persephone has now done). The stories belong together because each is about a middle-aged woman who takes sole responsibility for her children. The children are absorbed in their own young lives and have to be shielded from a parent's behaviour. Another thing we notice in each of them is the absence of direct confrontation. Mrs Blencarrow's story is dominated by voices speaking through the darkness, figures glimpsed in half-light. She and Brown, her husband, are never seen having a private conversation. We are never told how they fell in love or what went wrong. In the same way, we never get inside Mr Lycett-Landon's obsession with the young woman he cannot legally marry. Eleanor and the reader never know 'how the other story ended: if the poor Rose, her husband's unfortunate young wife, died of it, or if she abandoned him; or if the poor mother lacked the courage to tell her; or if between them the young woman was kept in her poor little suburban paradise deceived.' When her mother finds out the truth and faints, at the end of Chapter Nine, 'The Revelation', we are all set for a great scene in the next chapter. But it does not come.

Probably Margaret Oliphant felt that she had already told us as much as we needed to know. She had grown up believing strongly that there were certain things which respectable families did not discuss. She had had a brother (not Frank) who was an alcoholic and made her early life miserable; she grew used to covering up for him. She never discussed her marriage, or her chronic money problems, or her disappointments with her sons. All these things got into her fiction, but she refused to acknowledge them. 'Nothing before the children!' says Mrs Blencarrow, and Mrs Lycett-Landon's chief worry, when she discovers her husband's other life, is how to keep her children from knowing. 'Milly never heard till after her marriage what it was that had happened, and at no time did Horace ask any questions'. A suitable alternative name for this volume might be *Secrets and Lies*.

Merryn Williams
Oxford, 2010

If you have enjoyed this Persephone book why not telephone or write to us for a free copy of the Persephone Catalogue and the current Persephone Biannually? All Persephone books ordered from us cost £10 or three for £27 plus £2 postage per book.

PERSEPHONE BOOKS LTD
59 Lamb's Conduit Street
London WC1N 3NB

Telephone: 020 7242 9292
sales@persephonebooks.co.uk
www.persephonebooks.co.uk